"You have found my beloved daughter and brought her to me. Therefore, I will entrust her to you," the king said.

Rafe looked as if he'd just sucked a lemon. "Your Highness, I don't—"

The king cut him off. "My mind is made up. I will trust only you."

"Trust him for what?" Zara interjected.

"Rafe will be your bodyguard. He will protect you with his life."

Rafe held in a groan. He did *not* need this kind of trouble. Protecting royalty wasn't a big deal—but guarding the king of Bahania's newly found virgin daughter wasn't his idea of a good time. The king wouldn't want anyone messing with Princess Zara for *any* reason.

Which meant that, should Rafe be foolish enough to let his libido overrule his common sense, his secret attraction to Zara could be a one-way ticket to his beheading!

Dear Reader,

Spring is a time for new beginnings. And as you step out to enjoy the spring sunshine, I'd like to introduce a new author to Silhouette Special Edition. Her name is Judy Duarte, and her novel *Cowboy Courage* tells the heartwarming story of a runaway heiress who finds shelter in the strong arms of a handsome—yet guarded—cowboy. Don't miss this brilliant debut!

Next, we have the new installment in Susan Mallery's DESERT ROGUES miniseries. In *The Sheik & the Virgin Princess,* a beautiful princess goes in search of her long-lost royal father, and on her quest falls in love with her heart-meltingly gorgeous bodyguard! And love proves to be the irresistible icing in this adorable tale by Patricia Coughlin, *The Cupcake Queen.* Here, a lovable heroine turns her hero's life into a virtual beehive. But Cupid's arrow does get the final—er—sting!

I'm delighted to bring you Crystal Green's *His Arch Enemy's Daughter*, the next story in her poignant miniseries KANE'S CROSSING. When a rugged sheriff falls for the wrong woman, he has to choose between revenge and love. Add to the month Pat Warren's exciting new two-in-one, *My Very Own Millionaire*— two fabulous romances in one novel about confirmed bachelors who finally find the women of their dreams! Lastly, there is no shortage of gripping emotion (or tears!) in Lois Faye Dyer's *Cattleman's Bride-To-Be,* where long-lost lovers must reunite to save the life of a little girl. As they fight the medical odds, this hero and heroine find that passion—and soul-searing love—never die....

I'm so happy to present these first fruits of spring. I hope you enjoy this month's lineup and come back for next month's moving stories about life, love and family!

Best,

Karen Taylor Richman
Senior Editor

Please address questions and book requests to:
Silhouette Reader Service
U.S.: 3010 Walden Ave., P.O. Box 1325, Buffalo, NY 14269
Canadian: P.O. Box 609, Fort Erie, Ont. L2A 5X3

Susan Mallery

THE SHEIK
&
THE VIRGIN
PRINCESS

Silhouette®

SPECIAL EDITION™

Published by Silhouette Books

America's Publisher of Contemporary Romance

SILHOUETTE BOOKS

ISBN 0-373-24453-3

THE SHEIK & THE VIRGIN PRINCESS

Copyright © 2002 by Susan Macias-Redmond

Visit Silhouette at www.eHarlequin.com

Printed in U.S.A.

Books by Susan Mallery

SUSAN MALLERY

is the bestselling author of over forty books for Harlequin and Silhouette Books. She makes her home in the Pacific Northwest with her handsome prince of a husband and her two adorable-but-not-so-bright cats.

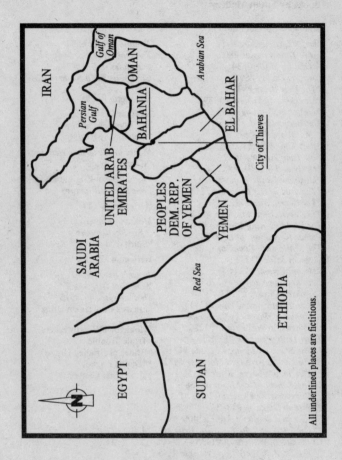

All underlined places are fictitious.

Chapter One

"What kind of stupid does it take *not* to want to be a princess?" Cleo asked.

Zara Paxton ignored both her sister and the question. Stupid or not, what she wanted more than anything was to turn tail and run. This had been a really bad idea from the start.

"The mosaics on the east wall date back to the early 1100s," the tour guide intoned as she pointed to the Bahanian palace wall covered with small tiles in a rainbow of colors. A few tiles had chipped over the past thousand years, but the majority were in place, detailing a lovely landscape of the ocean and a lush island in the distance.

"The scene is of Lucas-Surrat," the guide continued. "The crown prince of the island has always been a member of the Bahanian ruling family."

"How can you not want to know?" Cleo asked in a low voice. "Come on, Zara, take a chance."

"Easy for you to say," Zara pointed out. "We're not talking about your life."

"I wish we were. I would love to find out I'm the illegitimate daughter of royalty."

Zara hushed her sister, then glanced around to make sure that no one in their tour group had overheard Cleo's comments. Fortunately the others were more interested in what the guide had to say than any conversation between the two women.

Zara tugged on Cleo's arm, pulling her to a stop. "Don't say anything," she said urgently. "We're not sure what's true. So I have a few letters. They don't mean the king is really my father."

Cleo didn't look convinced. "If you don't think there's a possibility, what are we doing here?"

Zara didn't have an answer for that. The "here" in question was a public tour of the famous royal palace of Bahania. Cleo had suggested they simply announce themselves at the front gate and demand to be let in. Zara had opted for the more subtle approach—hence the tour. If nothing else, she could get the lay of the land, so to speak. Her trip to Bahania had been impulsive, something she tried to avoid. Now that she was here, she was going to have to think through what she wanted to do.

"You make me crazy," Cleo muttered, trailing after their group. "All your life you've wanted to know who your father is. You finally get some information on the man and suddenly you get all scared."

Zara shook her head. "You make it sound cut-and-dried, and it isn't. I thought my mother had an affair with a married man and that's why she wouldn't talk about my father. If it turns out he really *is* the king, then life is a whole lot more complicated. I'm not sure I want to be a part of all this.''

"Which brings me back to my stupid remark," Cleo said with a look of impatience. "Hello? This is your chance at the fairy tale, Zara. How many of us get to be transformed into a princess? Why on earth wouldn't you jump at the chance?"

"Because I—"

"Princess Sabra! I did not know you had arrived."

Both women turned to the man who hurried toward them. He was slight, in his mid-thirties and wearing some kind of uniform.

"I was told you would be arriving shortly. I had been watching for you, but must have missed you." The man stopped in front of them and bowed slightly. "A thousand pardons."

Zara blinked. "I'm sorry, but I have no idea what you're talking about. I'm not—"

"I am new," the man continued, as if she hadn't spoken. "Please do not be angry. This way."

Before Zara could protest, the man grabbed her arm and hustled her down a long corridor—one that led away from the tour group. She heard Cleo's footsteps as her sister hurried after her.

"Zara? What's going on?"

"I have no idea." She tried to free herself, but the little man's grip was surprisingly strong. "Look, you've made a mistake. I'm not who you think I am. I'm with the tour group. We're just tourists."

The man gave her a disapproving glance. "Yes, princess, but if you wanted a tour of the castle, you could simply ask your father, who is waiting for you even now."

Father? Zara's stomach tightened. She had a bad feeling about all of this.

They turned right, then left. She had a brief impression of large rooms, tile floors, beautiful statues and paintings, along with occasional glimpses of the blue Arabian Sea. Then they came to an oval foyer filled with half a dozen people. The man stopped and released her arm.

"I have found Princess Sabra," he announced to the milling crowd.

Everyone turned to look at her. Conversation stilled. In the heartbeat of silence, Zara knew that something awful was about to happen.

Her premonition proved true.

A male voice yelled that they were imposters. People dove at them from all directions. Zara didn't know what to do, and that indecision cost her breath when a large man threw himself at her. One second she was standing, the next she hit the hard, tiled floor with the impact of a train barreling into a brick wall.

Air rushed from her body. Her head banged against something unforgiving and the room began to spin. The next thing she knew, she couldn't breathe and there was a gun pointed at her temple.

"Talk!"

The voice commanded her obedience. Zara blinked and tried to suck in a breath. Her lungs wouldn't cooperate. The spinning increased, fueled by panic. She moved—or at least made the attempt—but her body froze. She inhaled again and this time air seeped into her lungs. Again and again she drew breath until she was able to focus. It was then that she realized her body wasn't frozen, it was pinned by a large, angry man with the coldest blue eyes she'd ever seen.

Blue had always been her favorite color, she thought somewhat hysterically. It was the color of the sea and the sky. But the irises of this man held no warmth. Staring at him, she felt chilled down to her bones. Maybe even down to her soul.

"Talk," he repeated. "Who the hell are you?"

"Zara Paxton," she breathed.

The pressure on her temple increased. She swallowed when she remembered the gun.

"Are you going to shoot me?" she asked, her voice shaking.

Everything she'd read about Bahania had told her that the country was safe, forward thinking and a perfect tourist destination. Perhaps the brochures had been wrong.

"What are you doing here?" he demanded, ignoring her question.

"My sister and I were touring the castle. A man pulled us away and insisted we come with him." She hesitated, not wanting to say that he'd called her Princess Sabra and had mentioned seeing the king. That sounded too far-fetched to be believed.

Those cold blue eyes never wavered from her face. She didn't doubt that he could read her every thought, so there was no need to go into detail. She noticed the man wore traditional Middle-Eastern garb, and that his Anglo features looked out of place.

They were nestled together intimately, his legs pinning hers, his chest flattening her breasts. One of his hands rested on her throat where he could no doubt feel the galloping of her pulse.

She licked her lips. "I'm sorry."

"Me, too," the man muttered as he slid off her and got to his feet.

Zara sat up slowly. She glanced around and saw that she was the center of attention—one of her least favorite things to be. Two burly guards were holding Cleo, but released her when the blue-eyed man instructed them to do so.

Zara got awkwardly to her feet. She still felt a little shaky and afraid. Cleo rushed to her side and they held each other. Zara pushed up her glasses.

"What happens now, Mr...." Her voice trailed off as she realized she didn't know the man's name.

"Rafe Stryker."

He spoke several sharp commands in a language she didn't recognize. The area cleared.

"Come this way," he said, and started walking without checking to see if they would follow.

Zara had the idle thought that they could run for it, but where would they go? They were in a strange country, in a huge castle and she had no idea of the floor plan. As the guards had disappeared, it seemed unlikely that they were about to be arrested.

She glanced at Cleo, who shrugged. Together the two women trailed after the man in the long robe and traditional headdress.

He led them into a small office. After seating them in chairs, he perched on the corner of the desk and studied them both.

"There's been some kind of misunderstanding," Zara said when the silence had stretched on for too long. "I was telling the truth before. My sister and I were on the tour, and suddenly we were dragged away. Then you and those guards attacked us. I'd like to know what's going on."

Rafe Stryker rubbed his temple. "That's what I'd like to know, as well. You two have any ID on you?"

Zara and Cleo exchanged a look. Did they really want to turn their passports over to this man?

"I'm not the bad guy here," Rafe said, confirming Zara's suspicions that he could read her mind. "I won't take any documents out of this room. I simply want to make a few phone calls."

"I don't think we have a choice," Cleo said in a stage whisper. Her short blond hair was more spiky than usual, and the corners of her full mouth trembled.

Zara nodded. She had been worried about a lot of things when they'd talked about coming to Bahania, but being attacked in the palace wasn't one of them. What on earth was going on?

They pulled their passports out of their purses and handed them over. Rafe picked up the phone on the desk and began making calls.

Five minutes later a young woman appeared with a tray of cold drinks and small sandwiches. She smiled as she entered and set the refreshments on the credenza by the window. Without saying a word, she bowed slightly and backed out of the room. Rafe was still talking, but he jerked his head toward the food.

Zara took that as a sign that it was permissible for them to partake of the offering. She and Cleo stood and moved to the far side of the room.

Cleo, always hungry, eyed the snack. "Think they're drugged?"

"I'm beginning to think we're caught up in a badly made spy movie," Zara admitted, trying to ignore the way she trembled. Adrenaline surged through her, making her want to run and hide. "But I doubt they went to all the trouble to drug the food."

Cleo shrugged and reached for one of the glasses. She sipped, then sighed. "Lemonade. It's perfect."

Zara's mouth watered and she found herself sipping the ice-cold liquid. While Cleo munched on a tiny sandwich, Zara studied the small office, along with their host.

The room was modern, with a computer against the far wall and a fax machine. The only window overlooked a courtyard filled with a garden of different flowers and fruit trees. Linoleum covered the floor, not the tiles they'd seen on their palace tour.

Her gaze slipped back to the man on the phone. Zara couldn't tell much about his body due to the long flowing robe covering him, but she'd felt his strength as he'd pressed into her, holding her captive. His accent sounded American. He had blue eyes, and while his skin was tanned it wasn't dark. What was Rafe Stryker doing in the Bahanian royal palace and why was he pulling guns on unsuspecting tourists?

As if sensing her attention, Rafe turned toward her.

Zara told herself to look away. Even as a blush climbed her cheeks, she couldn't seem to make herself move. It was as if he'd mesmerized her. Her body stilled, her heartbeat slowed, and once again she could feel the weight of him on top of her.

No emotion flickered in his eyes. His firm mouth didn't give away his feelings, nor did his body language.

Finally he shifted and hung up the phone. Zara felt as if she'd been released from a spell. The shivering returned, along with the sensation of being exposed.

"So what's a nice schoolteacher like you doing in a place like Bahania?" Rafe asked.

His voice—deep and strong—made her swallow. "I'm not a schoolteacher, I'm a college professor."

He shrugged as if to say "what's the difference?"

Cleo sighed. "Zara worked her butt off to get to full professor. You'd better not mess with her about that."

Cleo made her announcement in between sandwiches. When Rafe turned his steady gaze to her, Cleo instantly took a step back.

"I mean it," she said sounding brazen, all retreats to the contrary. "For all we know, her father is the king. You don't want to get him mad at you, right?"

"King Hassan is your father?"

Rafe asked the question with just enough amusement to make Zara wince. She put down her drink and squared her shoulders. This had gone on long enough.

"Here's what I know. My sister and I are American citizens on a public tour of the palace. For reasons no one has explained, we were forcibly taken away from our tour and led into a private area. There we were attacked. Now you've taken possession of our passports. I want them returned immediately, then I would like us to be escorted from the palace.''

"Zara!'' Cleo frowned. "What about the king?''

"This isn't the time,'' she said, not looking at her sister, instead focusing on Rafe Stryker, who hadn't appeared the least bit impressed by her speech.

He surprised her by holding out their passports. But other than that, he didn't make any attempt to grant her wishes.

Zara grabbed the documents and tucked them into her purse. "May we leave now?'' she asked.

"Not until I hear the whole story.''

"There isn't a story.''

"There's the letters,'' Cleo said helpfully. "Zara has these letters from King Hassan to her mother.''

Rafe carefully watched the two sisters. Cleo, the younger, was short and blond, with the curvy kind of figure that made most men's mouths water. Rafe dismissed her. He was far more interested in the tall, slender brunette who claimed to be the daughter of a king.

He could see how the guard had mistaken her for Princess Sabra. Zara was only a couple of inches taller. Her coloring was the same, as were her features. Both she and the princess had large brown eyes, and the shape of their faces was remarkably similar. However, the American schoolteacher wore glasses, while the princess did not. And even though he'd been in close contact with Princess Sabra, never once had his body reacted to her. However, his few moments of nearness to Zara Paxton had left him... intrigued.

Zara sighed. She pulled the chair a couple of feet away from the desk, then settled onto the seat. Still holding her lemonade, she reached into her large purse and drew out a stack of letters.

"My mother never told me who my father was. There were no pictures, no personal effects. She didn't even share many stories about their time together. I assumed he was a wealthy married man. You see, she'd been a dancer and very beautiful. Men were always interested in her."

Zara smiled slightly, as if remembering something that brought her pleasure. The smile faded as she fingered the letters.

"There were several pieces of jewelry. My mother sold most of them over the years to supplement our income. She died eight years ago, and I figured that any information about my father died with her."

"Why did you come here now?" he asked, even as he wondered how much she intended to ask for. Had the plan been her idea or her sister's? At what point had she realized she had more than a passing resemblance to Princess Sabra, and when had she decided to use that to her advantage?

"My mother kept these letters along with several other personal mementos with an attorney. I only discovered their existence a few months ago when he sent a bill for storage. I requested the things be sent to me instead. Once I read them, I realized..." Her voice trailed off.

"That you might be the king's daughter. May I see the letters?"

Zara shook her head. "You know what I'd really like?"

About five million dollars, Rafe thought cynically.

"I'd like to go back to my hotel and forget this ever happened."

"What?" Cleo sounded outraged.

Zara ignored her. "There's been a mistake. I don't want to be here. Can you get us out of the palace?"

Rafe considered the possibilities. Either she was having second thoughts about her plan, or she wanted time to come up with a better story. Or she was preparing to go to the media. Better that he not let her wander around on her own just yet.

"How about if I take you back to your hotel myself? As a way of apologizing?"

"Just show us the nearest exit and we'll be fine."

"I'd prefer to escort you. I insist."

Zara didn't look too happy, but she nodded her agreement. Rafe excused himself while he went to change his clothes, promising to return in ten minutes.

"What are you doing?" Cleo asked the second they were alone. "Why do you want to go back to the hotel? Zara, this is your chance to meet the king."

Zara set her drink on the desk, rose and paced to the window. "Don't you get it? Couldn't you tell by the way he was looking at us? Rafe thinks we're here for money."

Cleo grinned. "Isn't that one of the perks of being a princess?"

"I'm serious. He doesn't believe us. He thinks we're going to blackmail the king or something. It's horrible." She folded her arms over her chest.

All the times she'd imagined coming to Bahania, she tried to think of everything that could go wrong. She'd pictured the king telling her she wasn't his daughter. She'd thought about having him admit to being her father and not wanting anything to do with her. She'd even figured he might think she was crazy. But she'd never thought anyone would think she was in it for the money.

"Why couldn't Mom have fallen in love with a banker or an executive? Why did it have to be the King of Bahania?"

Cleo didn't bother to respond. Zara knew her sister thought she was crazy for not simply marching up to the king and announcing she was his long-lost daughter. As if Zara had any chance of getting close to a member of the royal family. Besides, Cleo didn't understand her ambivalence about the whole situation. Things had looked a lot clearer from five thousand miles away.

The door opened and Rafe entered. "Are you two ready?" he asked.

Cleo glared at Zara, as if daring her to say they could go. Which was unnecessary, because Zara wasn't in a position to speak. In his traditional headdress and robes Rafe had been tall and intimidating. Dressed in a well-cut business suit, he was simply gorgeous.

His gold-blond hair had been cut military short, a style that looked both severe and sexy. He had a strong jaw, a perfect mouth, and while his eyes were still cold enough to freeze air, they were also doing odd things to Zara's insides.

She'd never felt herself melting in the mere presence of a man. But even as she stood there, she could feel her bones dissolving. It was impossible to move, let alone have a coherent thought.

She'd come halfway around the world to find the man who might be her father. In the space of an hour, she'd had second, third and fourth thoughts, been thrown to the ground, held at gunpoint, accused of being a gold digger and struck by lightning. All this and it wasn't even noon.

Chapter Two

"Cool! A limo!"

Cleo beamed with excitement as they exited the palace through a side door and saw the waiting transportation. Zara tried to work up an equal amount of energy at the thought of riding in such an expensive car for the first time in her life. Unfortunately, all her extra attention was focused on continuing to breathe. Being too close to dangerous, not to mention mysterious, Rafe Stryker left her gasping.

What was wrong with her, Zara wondered. Why was she reacting this way to the man? Yes, he'd attacked her, throwing her to the ground, and that would have rattled anyone. But she should be over it by now. Unless her brain had somehow been scrambled during the altercation. Maybe that was it—she had a brain bruise.

Cleo slipped into the limo first. Unfortunately, she took the seat behind the driver, which left Zara to slide across the seat facing front. Rafe settled next to her. She scooted all the way to the corner so there would be plenty of room between them. She needed the distance to keep her thoughts from scattering.

"I should have stayed home," she said aloud, before she could stop herself.

Rafe glanced at her. "It's too late now."

She didn't want to think about that. The car pulled away from the palace. Cleo leaned forward and stared out the darkened window.

"It really is pink," she said, her voice laced with awe. "I read that people call it the pink palace when we were doing our research, but I thought they were kidding."

"It's an effect of the marble," Rafe told Cleo. "Something about the way the light hits it."

"I like it," Cleo announced. She leaned back in her seat, one hand stroking the supple leather. "I just wish we'd seen some of the royal cats while we'd been on the tour. We read about those, too. Does the king really keep dozens of cats in the palace?"

Rafe nodded. "They are considered a national treasure."

"Lucky cats," Cleo said, and grinned at Zara.

Zara tried to respond in kind, but her lips weren't cooperating. She'd barely managed to slow her heart rate to something other than the speed of light. Now she concentrated on taking deep, cleansing breaths.

"How did you do your research?" Rafe asked.

Cleo shrugged, her pretty face completely open.

''Mostly on the Internet. Zara's at the University, so she looked in some books there, but I checked online. I have Internet access at my work. It was pretty easy. There's a ton of information on the history of the country and the royal family. We downloaded pictures and everything.''

Zara winced. Cleo was only making things worse, but Zara couldn't tell her that. Not in front of Rafe. He'd already decided they were gold diggers. Now he would think they were using technology to gather information to aid their scheme. Not that she could blame him. If she looked at the situation from his point of view there really wasn't another explanation.

It was time to go home, Zara thought. She'd been crazy to think this would ever work. Even if King Hassan was her father, she wasn't likely to have any contact with him—there would be too many watchdogs in place. She'd survived twenty-eight years without a father; she certainly didn't need one now.

The limo pulled up in front of their hotel. Zara remembered neither she nor Cleo had told Rafe where they were staying. The realization that he could get that information so easily made her shiver and reinforced her decision to leave. She wanted to go home where she felt safe. In Bahania she would only ever be out of place.

Rafe climbed out first, then held the door open for them. Zara forced herself to be gracious as she thanked him for the ride.

''You've been very kind,'' she said. ''We won't be troubling you again.''

But he didn't climb back into the car. Instead he

took her arm and led her into the modest hotel. "I think we have more to discuss," he said, not giving her an opportunity to protest. Cleo trailed along behind.

Zara made one attempt to pull free of his grip, but as she'd suspected, he didn't let her go. No doubt he wanted to scare them into leaving. As soon as they were in private, she would tell him that he didn't have to worry. She and Cleo would be heading back to the States as soon as possible.

They moved through the lobby toward the elevator. Zara tried not to notice the clean but slightly shabby furniture. Prints added color to the white walls. There were a few plants scattered around, but little else in the way of decorations.

She knew what he was thinking. She could read his thoughts as clearly as if they were her own.

"Just because we're on a budget doesn't mean we're in it for the money," she said in a low, angry voice when they stopped for the elevator. "You have no right to judge me or find me wanting."

Those amazing blue eyes turned toward her. She met his gaze, despite the powerful force he exuded. Pride stiffened her spine and made her strong.

The elevator doors opened, breaking the spell.

"So do you know the king?" Cleo asked, oblivious to the tension between them.

"Yes."

She laughed. "You're not real chatty, are you? It doesn't matter how mad you want to be. The truth is Zara is his daughter. She has letters and a ring. I think you should do your darnedest to prove them to be fakes. When you can't, you'll have no choice but to accept her for who she says she is."

For the first time since they were led away from the tour group, Zara felt herself relax. Maybe it was a little too soon to think about running away.

"You have an excellent point," she told her sister.

"I *am* more than a pretty face," Cleo reminded her, as the elevator came to a stop on the fourth floor.

Zara turned to the man who still had a death grip on her arm. "Are you willing to look at the evidence? Despite already reaching a conclusion?"

"Absolutely."

"And when you find out you're wrong?"

"Let's discuss that if it happens."

Thirty minutes later Rafe was less convinced this was a hoax. He fingered the dozen or so letters Zara had shown him. The subject matter—especially the comments about the cats—made him suspicious. All the information could have been gathered by careful research. However the handwriting looked like Hassan's, and the syntax was pure royal-speak. But what convinced him the most was the feeling in his gut.

Long years of experience had taught him to listen to his instincts—instincts that had saved his life on more than one occasion. He fingered the yellowing linen paper, then glanced at the stack of letters on the small desk in the hotel room. Despite his assumptions that Zara and her sister were looking to make an easy couple of million, there was a good chance he'd been wrong.

"Anything else?" he asked, turning his attention to the woman sitting on the bed next to the desk.

Zara reached into her carry-on bag and drew out a pad of paper. "Here's a list of the jewelry I can remember my mother selling. It's not a complete list because I'm sure she sold some before I was born or while I was too young to know what was happening. There's also this."

The "this" turned out to be a diamond band inscribed with the word *forever* on the inside. The tightening in Rafe's gut got worse.

Zara sat facing him, her hands carefully folded on her lap. She wore a light cotton, peach sundress and sandals. Her long hair tumbled down her back. With her dark eyes and honeyed complexion, she looked a lot like Princess Sabra—Sabrina—the king's only daughter.

Yeah, there were differences. Sabrina didn't wear glasses and she had an air of confidence that Zara lacked. Still, the combination of the physical similarities and the evidence made him fairly sure Zara was exactly who she claimed to be. He couldn't begin to imagine what was going to happen when the king found out.

"What stories did your mother tell you about your father?" he asked.

"She rarely said anything." Zara shrugged. "When I would ask questions, she would just say that they couldn't be together. He didn't know about me and she wasn't in a position to tell me about him. I used to ask if he would want me if he found out he had a daughter. She always said he would, but I never knew if that was her interpretation of events or if it was true.''

The information hardly helped. He glanced over at Cleo who had stretched out on the far bed, reading a fashion magazine.

''Do you remember your mother telling any stories about your father?''

Cleo smiled. ''I'm not lucky enough to be related to royalty. Sorry.''

''Cleo is my foster sister,'' Zara said.

''That's right. Fiona brought me home when I was ten, just like picking up a puppy in a pound. I was housebroken, so she decided to keep me.''

Cleo spoke cheerfully enough, but there was a hint of darkness in her eyes. Rafe studied her pretty round face, taking in the wide eyes, blond hair and full, pouty mouth. She didn't look anything like Zara.

Zara glared at her sister. ''It wasn't quite like that. Cleo came to us as a foster child, but quickly became a member of the family.''

This was more information than Rafe had wanted. ''So you're not blood relatives.''

Zara returned her attention to him. ''No.'' She opened her mouth as if she was about to speak, then shook her head and rose. ''I can't do this,'' she said, and headed for the balcony.

Cleo sighed. ''Zara's been like this since we left Spokane,'' she confided. ''It's one thing to say you want to meet your real father, but it's another to have it happen. At least, that's what she says. I think being related to royalty is pretty cool, but then, Zara's always been the sensitive one.''

Sensitive? Rafe didn't do sensitive. Why the hell had he been the one standing in the room when the guard had brought in Zara? Couldn't someone else have attacked her and been responsible for this mess?

Muttering under his breath, he rose and stalked out to the small balcony that overlooked the tourist portion of the city. The late-May heat was a tangible creature, sucking air from his lungs and moisture from his body. Zara didn't seem to notice as she leaned against the railing and stared off into the distance.

"I don't want you to say anything to the king," she said without looking at him.

"I don't have a choice."

That got her attention. She spun toward him. "Why? It doesn't matter. He already has one daughter…he doesn't need another one. Besides, I don't think I'd be a very good princess."

"You'd be fine."

Rafe shifted uneasily. He didn't like emotional confrontations with women who looked as if they might start to cry.

She swallowed. "You think maybe he's really…" Her voice trailed off as she gestured to the letters he still held in his hand.

He knew what she was asking. "Yes, Zara. I think he could be your father."

She turned her attention back to the city. "I didn't think it would be like this," she said quietly. "All my life I've wanted to belong to a real family. To have relatives and roots. But not here—with royalty. I wanted some normal, American family. You know the kind with a bunch of kids and maybe one or two eccentric relatives.''

She had a perfect profile. His gaze lingered on the gentle curve of her mouth and the length of her neck. Something flickered inside. Something that had nothing to do with his gut instincts and everything to do with being a man.

A faint breeze stirred, bringing with it the scent of her. A scent he remembered from when he'd attacked her. Even as he'd pulled a gun and prepared to defend the royal house of Bahania, he'd been aware of her feminine fragrance, not to mention her body beneath his.

She looked at him. ''What if I can't do this?''

There were questions in her brown eyes. Questions and pain.

''I could act as intermediary,'' he found himself saying. ''I could take the letters and the ring to the king privately. You wouldn't have to be there, and no one else would have to know.''

She bit her lower lip. ''Once you begin, there's no turning back. I don't like that.''

''You wouldn't have come here if you hadn't wanted this,'' he reminded her. ''You're the one who started this in motion by going to the palace.''

''But wanting and getting are too different things. Maybe Cleo and I should just disappear.''

''If you do, you'll spend the rest of your life wondering what would have happened.''

''Maybe that doesn't sound so bad.'' Zara hesitated, then nodded. ''You're right. I'm here. I want to know the truth. If you wouldn't mind taking the letters to the king, that would be great. I'm not feeling brave enough to be rejected in person. Not that I could get in to see the king."

Rafe didn't know how the king was going to react, but he was fairly certain Hassan was Zara's father. Which could create many complications.

She headed toward the room. "You should probably take the ring, too."

She was so damn trusting. "How do you know I'll return it?"

She stopped to stare at him. "Why would you keep it?"

He groaned. "You have no business traveling on your own."

"I'm not. I'm with my sister."

"The blind leading the blind."

She drew herself up to her full height and glared at him. As he was six foot three, the top of her head barely grazed his chin. He wasn't impressed by her erect posture or the fire spitting from her eyes.

"Cleo and I have done perfectly well without your help."

"I can see that. Getting attacked at the palace was part of your plan all along, right?"

"That was your fault, not mine."

"In a situation like this you have to be prepared for the unexpected." Although she'd certainly caught *him* off guard.

Zara's temper faded. "Do I really look like her?"

"Enough to fool a new guard."

"But not you."

"No." He shifted from foot to foot. "I'm sorry I attacked you."

"It's all right. You thought there was a threat."

Looking at her now he didn't see how that was possible, but that was what he'd assumed.

She pushed up her glasses. "Do you think there's really a chance I'm the king's daughter?"

"What do you know about your name?" he asked instead of answering her question.

"Nothing. I mean I know it's unusual, but if you'd ever met my mother, you wouldn't be surprised. She wasn't exactly the most conventional person on the planet."

"Zara was King Hassan's mother's name."

Zara shivered, as if she were suddenly cold. Rafe didn't blame her. She might have come to Bahania looking for her father, but she was about to get a whole lot more than she'd bargained for.

Zara paced restlessly after Rafe left. "He said he'd call as soon as he saw the king," she said, more to herself than to Cleo, who was still reading her magazine. "He said he could get in to see him this afternoon. What kind of man can just waltz in and see the king?"

"A man with connections," Cleo said, then grinned at her. "Honey, you're taking this way too hard. What's the worst that can happen? You'll turn out not to be Hassan's daughter. Then we can enjoy the rest of our vacation and head home."

Zara supposed it was just that simple, although there was a part of her that hated the idea of being fatherless again. Not that she wanted a king for her father.

"I didn't think it would be so complicated," she admitted, more to herself than to Cleo.

"It's not so complicated. Nothing's changed."

Zara sank onto her bed and shook her head. Things *had* changed the second Rafe Stryker had tossed her to the ground. Not only was she seeing their position from someone else's point of view, she couldn't stop thinking about his incredible blue eyes and how her insides quivered when she was close to him.

"Who do you think he is?" she asked. "Rafe was dressed like a sheik, but he's obviously American."

"What does it matter, as long as he can do what he says." Cleo tossed the magazine aside and rolled toward her. "Forget about him. Think about the palace instead. Wouldn't it be great to live there? It was so beautiful."

"It was big and scary," Zara said.

Cleo sighed. "What am I going to do with you? This is a fabulous opportunity and you're going to blow it by getting cold feet. We're talking princess, Zara. You could be an honest-to-goodness princess. That doesn't happen to people like us. It wasn't that long ago that money was so tight we could only afford day-old bread."

"I know."

"You could be rich."

"I don't want to be rich—I want to belong. I want roots and relatives and a history."

"You could have all of that and a tiara, too."

Zara laughed. "Is that all you can think about?"

Cleo grinned. "Diamonds have a way of getting my attention."

"You talk big, but in your heart you want what I want. Real family."

"Maybe, but I'd settle for royalty."

Zara tucked her legs under her. "Do you think Rafe works for the king?"

Cleo groaned. "Don't you dare get all dopey about that guy. For one thing, you're about to find out if the king of a wealthy nation is your father. You don't have time to be distracted. Second, you have the worst luck on the planet when it comes to men. Don't even think about it."

"I know."

Zara couldn't disagree with either of her sister's statements. She just might be starting an amazing adventure, and her ill fortune with men bordered on legendary. Still there'd been something about Rafe's eyes.

"I wonder if he's married," she murmured.

Cleo threw a pillow at her. "Stop it. Think about being a princess instead."

"All right."

But as Zara shifted to stretch out on the bed, she pictured a tall, dangerous looking man with a gaze that seemed to see into her soul.

Chapter Three

Instead of going directly to the king, Rafe detoured by his own office first. Once there he headed for his computer, prepared to research the possibility of Zara Paxton being King Hassan's illegitimate daughter.

A part of him had already accepted her story, which made him uneasy. Except for the feeling in his gut, he had no reason to trust her. Was he getting soft? Had he been out of combat too long? Or were his instincts telling him the truth?

Forty minutes later he had a rough idea of the king's travel schedule from thirty years ago. There weren't a lot of details, but it was obvious that Hassan had frequently visited New York City. Rafe toyed with the idea of breaking into the financial records to check on jewelry purchases, but figured he would do better to ask the king directly.

Rafe reached for the ring he'd slipped into his pocket and turned it over in his hand. The diamonds glinted in the midafternoon light. They circled the entire band. Again he studied the inscription of the word *forever*. Had the king meant the sentiment? He'd never been one to keep a mistress or wife around for very long. He had only ever loved one of his three wives. Had Zara's mother been the only other woman to truly capture the monarch's heart?

There was only one way to find out.

Rafe called Hassan's secretary and requested a few minutes for a private meeting. Fortunately, the king was running ahead of schedule. Rafe collected the letters, tucked the ring back into his pocket and headed for the rear of the palace.

His Highness, the king of Bahania, believed in first impressions. His office suite was the size of a football field and overlooked a topiary garden growing around a large white fountain. Four guards in formal dress stood in front of wide double doors overlaid with a gold coat of arms. Once inside the suite, three secretaries protected the king from those who wished to see him. Two-story-high windows overlooked the lush gardens surrounding the palace, while priceless works of art hung on the walls—both paintings and tapestries delighting the eye. And wandering around as if they owned the place were several cats.

Rafe nodded at the guards as he approached. They opened the outer doors for him. As he entered, a white Persian cat slipped out, pausing to rub against him long enough to deposit several white hairs on his trousers. Rafe gritted his teeth. He'd never been much of a cat kind of guy—he was a dog person. But this was

not the place to mention that. The king adored his
cats.

Two gray cats lay curled up on a sofa by the window. A calico had stretched out on one of the secretaries' desk, using a stack of files for a pillow. Rafe
ignored the felines and approached the center desk.

Akil, an older man who had served the king for
many years, smiled in greeting. "Mr. Stryker. His
Highness is waiting for you. Please go on in."

Rafe touched his suit pocket to make sure the ring
was still in place, then headed for the half-open door
on the left. As he entered the king of Bahania's private chambers, he bowed.

"Your Highness," he said, and paused.

King Hassan sat behind an impressive hand carved
desk. The king generally wore Western-style suits
during his working day and today was no exception.
The tailored lightweight wool garment had been made
by hand in Italy, the fabric especially woven to resist
the ever-present cat hairs shed by the monarch's beloved felines.

"Rafe, what brings you to see me?" Hassan asked,
waving his guest forward.

Rafe had to move a dozing Siamese from a chair
before he could sit and was then forced to allow the
animal to drape itself across his lap. He couldn't wait
to get back to his regular job. At least *his* boss didn't
have a thing for cats.

"I have an unusual situation to report," Rafe began.

Hassan raised his eyebrows. The king was close to
sixty, but still a youthful-looking man. A few gray
hairs had appeared in his closely trimmed beard but
there weren't many wrinkles on his face. He could be

stern and distant. Until the recent decision to form a
joint air force between Bahania, neighboring El Bahar
and the City of Thieves, Rafe had had little to do with
the king. Acting as the security liaison for the City of
Thieves had recently put Rafe in close contact with
the ruler of Bahania. He had yet to form an opinion
of the man, so he couldn't predict his reaction to
Rafe's news.

Hassan leaned forward. "Situation? With security?"

"No. This is personal. I haven't discussed this with
anyone, sir. If you instruct me to keep this to myself,
I will never speak of it again."

Hassan smiled slightly. "I'm intrigued. Go on."

Rafe hesitated. He was about to tread over some
potentially dangerous waters. "A young woman came
to the palace this morning. She was part of the regular
public tour. One of the guards noticed her because
she bears a striking resemblance to the Princess Sabra."

Hassan nodded to show he was listening. So far he
hadn't reacted. Rafe continued.

"I spoke with the young woman in question."
He'd already decided not to mention the details of
their meeting. "She recently discovered some papers
which had belonged to her late mother. Letters, actually. She thinks they may have been written by
you."

Hassan's face tightened. "Who is this woman?
How old is she?"

"Her name is Zara Paxton. She's twenty-eight."

Hassan gasped as if he'd been shot. He held out
his hands for the letters, and as Rafe passed them over
he already had his answer. Hassan looked both elated

and stunned. Both the name and the age had been significant to him.

While the king was distracted with the pages, he took the opportunity to set the cat on the ground and brush the hair from his lap.

Hassan opened each letter slowly and read it, then put it back in the envelope. Color drained from his face. When he'd finished, Rafe gave him the diamond ring. The king took it and closed his fingers around the stones.

"Fiona," he breathed, then looked at Rafe. "The daughter. Where is she?"

"Zara is staying at a hotel in the city. Her mother died some years ago. Apparently, she had kept these letters with a lawyer. Zara only found out about them a few months ago. She thinks you could be her father."

Hassan rose, with Rafe quickly doing the same. "Of course she is my daughter. Fiona and I were together for over two years. After all this time her daughter is here. My daughter." He shook his head. "You say she looks like Sabrina?"

"They have the same coloring, the same general build. Zara is taller and thinner. She wears glasses."

Hassan smiled sadly, obviously caught up in a memory. "My sweet Fiona was as blind as a bat, but vain. She would never wear her glasses. I used to have to lead her everywhere." He headed for the door. "Come. I must meet Zara at once."

Rafe grabbed the letters—Hassan still had the ring. "Your Highness, we need to talk about this first."

The king turned to face him. "Why?"

"For one thing, you can't know if she's really your daughter."

''True enough, although I suspect she is.''

He wanted her to be. Rafe read that truth in the longing in Hassan's dark eyes. Rafe felt oddly protective of the woman he'd left back in the hotel.

''Zara is a little nervous about the situation. She's not prepared to have her long-lost father be the king of a sizable country. There's also the problem of the media. Until we know who she is, it's best if we keep this information private.''

''I see your point.'' Hassan nodded slowly. ''What do you suggest?''

''A meeting in a neutral location. One of the big hotels, maybe. We can use one of the suites. Your security people can get you into the building quietly. I'll bring Zara.''

Hassan glanced at his watch. ''Have this arranged by four o'clock. I won't wait any longer.''

Which gave Rafe less than two hours. Great. ''Yes, Your Highness. I'll take care of everything.''

''I'm going to throw up,'' Zara announced as she stood in the center of the massive living room of the presidential suite at the Bahanian Resort Hotel.

To her left were floor-to-ceiling windows overlooking the incredible Arabian Ocean. She'd already tried concentrating on the view as a way to calm herself, but the height made her head swim...and not in a good way.

The furniture in the suite was enough to make her uneasy. The living room held five sofas—five!—and a baby grand piano. There were also coffee tables and sofa tables. All this furniture, and there was still enough floor space to hold an aerobics class.

She and Cleo had yet to find their way through the

entire suite. They'd gotten lost twice then had given up exploring, fearing that the king would arrive and find them trapped in a bedroom closet or bathroom.

"Don't throw up," Cleo advised. "It never makes a good first impression."

"Thanks for the share." Zara tried for a smile, but her face felt frozen and tight. Like she'd had too much Novocain at the dentist. "What are we doing here? Are we crazy?"

Cleo rubbed her hand along the back of one of the sofas. "I don't know, Zara. I mean, I didn't really connect this whole king-father thing before. But now it's real and it's scary."

"Tell me about it." Zara forced herself to sit. She chose a sofa that faced away from the windows. "At least Rafe arranged for us to meet the king here rather than at our hotel."

Cleo managed a brief smile. "I'll bet he's never been in a two-star place before. Do you want to know that you're the color of a sheet?"

"Not really." Her stomach tightened. "What was I thinking?"

"That it would be nice to meet the family." Cleo sank into a sofa opposite hers.

"You're my family," Zara reminded her. "Whatever happens here, I want you to know that. Anything else is just gravy."

Cleo rolled her eyes. "If your father turns out to be the king, then I would say that at least rates him being an entrée. Oh, and if you are a real princess, I want you to promise to send your jewelry castoffs my way."

Zara chuckled. "Deal. When my tiaras get old and dusty, I'll toss them your way."

"Cool. I could wear them to work."

The thought of Cleo wearing a diamond tiara while working at the copy shop she managed eased a lot of Zara's tension. She'd nearly relaxed enough to sit back in the sofa when the main door of the suite opened. Instantly her heart beelined for her throat and her entire body began to quiver.

"I can't," she breathed.

Cleo was at her side in a second, putting her arm around her and hugging her. "You can. If you have to throw up, rush for that plant and I'll distract him with a knock-knock joke."

Cleo's outrageous instructions allowed Zara to suck in a breath and get to her feet. Rafe entered the room, followed by a man she recognized from the research she'd done. A man who was staring at her as if she were the most amazing creature on the planet.

The dark intensity of his gaze made her uncomfortable. Was this really happening? Was the handsome, older man really King Hassan of Bahania?

"Your Highness, may I present Miss Zara Paxton," Rafe said, gesturing toward her.

Zara felt, more than saw, Cleo move away. She was vaguely aware of two more men entering the room. Security, she thought hazily, all of her attention focusing on the man who might be her father.

He was a few inches shorter than Rafe, but a couple of inches taller than her. He wore a suit and looked fit. His eyes were the same rich brown as her own, and when he smiled she thought she recognized the shape of his mouth.

"My long-lost daughter," he intoned, stepping toward her and holding out his arms. "The child of my beloved Fiona. Welcome. Welcome home."

Before she knew what was happening, she found herself caught up in the king's arms, pulled against him and held tight. Zara tried to hug him back, but she couldn't move. For the second time in one day, a strange man held her immobile.

She needed to escape, she thought frantically, and glanced around the room. Only Rafe seemed to notice her distress. He eased forward and gently disentangled the king.

"Perhaps we should all have a seat and discuss what has happened," he said, urging Hassan toward a sofa.

"Yes, yes." The king took hold of Zara's hand and sat down.

Zara perched next to him feeling both uneasy and awkward. He was royalty. Was she supposed to bow or sit lower or what? She looked to Rafe for an answer, but he was busy settling Cleo across from them, then he picked up the phone and announced that it was time to serve the refreshments.

Zara returned her attention to the king only to find him staring at her. His attention made her feel even more nervous. She pulled her fingers free of his and carefully laced her hands together.

"I don't know what to say," she admitted. "This is very strange. I'm sure Rafe explained about the letters. I don't mean to be presumptuous or to get in the way. I'm simply trying to find out some information."

Hassan sighed. "I see your mother in you. She was a true beauty. The most glorious rose in the garden of womanhood."

Zara blinked and pushed up her glasses. While Fiona *had* always been lovely, Zara had inherited little of her physical attributes and none of her charm. "Yes, well, I am tall like her." She glanced at Cleo. "Oh, you haven't met my sister. This is Cleo."

Cleo grinned. "Foster sister," she corrected. "Although I wouldn't mind being able to say my daddy is a king, I won't be able to claim that relationship."

Hassan chuckled. "I welcome you to my country. Is this your first visit?"

"For both of us. It's great. A little hot, but hey, that's why they invented air-conditioning." Cleo leaned forward. "I confess, you're the first royal person I've ever met. How exactly am I supposed to address you?"

"Your Highness is the accepted form," Rafe said hastily as someone knocked on the door.

The security guys went on instant alert. One of them headed for the door while the second one covered him. They stepped into the hallway for a minute, then reappeared pushing a tray of drinks and snacks.

"Now that's just what happens when I go through a fast-food drive through," Cleo murmured.

Hassan raised his eyebrows. "What is that?"

"You know. When you desperately want a burger and fries, but you don't want to get out of your car? You can place the order and pay, then get your food, never once putting out more effort than rolling down the window. You have to try it."

Hassan asked Cleo a few more questions. Zara admired her ability to be almost normal, despite the situation, then remembered that Cleo had a whole lot less on the line.

Rafe and the security men put the drinks and trays of snacks on the coffee table between the two sofas. Zara reached for a cola bottle, but her hands were shaking too much for her to unscrew the top. Rafe took the plastic bottle from her and unfastened it, then poured the fizzing liquid over a glass of ice.

"You're doing great," he said as he handed her the drink.

She hoped he was telling the truth. The urge to throw up hadn't gone away.

Hassan removed Fiona's diamond ring from his coat pocket and held it out. "I gave this to your mother on our one-year anniversary. I wanted to make sure she would never forget me."

"I don't think that was a problem," Zara said, then cleared her throat. "Your Highness, this is all very strange to me. I think, before we go too far, we should find out if I'm really your daughter."

"I already know. You look very much like Sabrina."

"Who?"

"Princess Sabra. She prefers the American version of her name."

Zara remembered the guard at the palace. "Okay, so I look like her. That doesn't prove anything."

"You have this." He placed the ring in her hand and closed her fingers over it. "I know, Zara. Here." He touched his chest. "That is all that matters."

Rafe sat next to Cleo and took a soda for himself.

Hassan touched Zara's cheek. "Your mother was younger than you are now when we met. I was young, as well. Very proud and certain of myself. I was visiting New York and wanted to see a Broadway show. Afterward, at a party, I met the cast. Your mother had captured my attention from the first moment she stepped onstage. I arranged for us to have a private introduction. She was as charming as she was beautiful. I believe I fell in love with her that first night.''

Zara had tried to be sensible and stay in control of her emotions, but hearing about her mother's past tested her resolve. Fiona had rarely talked about that time in her life and never said anything about the man who had fathered her child.

''I've seen a few pictures from when she was a showgirl,'' she admitted. ''She was lovely.''

''More than that. She had dozens of admirers, but from the first there was something special between us. We only wanted each other. We were together whenever I could get away.'' He smiled sadly. ''I asked her to marry me, but she refused.''

''Are you kidding?'' Cleo blurted, then covered her mouth. ''Sorry.''

Hassan shrugged. ''I was stunned, as well. However, I already had a wife. I offered to divorce her, but Fiona refused. She said she didn't want to make trouble and she doubted that she would have been content to live in one place, even one as amazing as Bahania.''

''My mother did like to wander,'' Zara said, a little dazed by all she was hearing. A king had offered to marry Fiona and she had said no?

Hassan studied her. ''Was there…'' He cleared his throat. ''I often wondered who Fiona had married.''

''She didn't,'' Zara said quickly. ''We moved around constantly and while Fiona always had dozens of friends, there was never a special man in her life. She used to tell me that she'd already fallen in love once and didn't plan to do it again.''

Hassan closed his eyes briefly. ''Yes. I gave her my heart, and when she left, she took it with her. I like to think she experienced the same with me. Perhaps not. We'll never know.'' He turned his attention back to Zara. ''At the time I could not understand why she disappeared from my world, but now I know. She must have left as soon as she found out she was pregnant. She knew that I would have insisted we marry. Even if we had not, she feared for her child.''

Too much was happening too fast. Zara felt as if her head was already too full of information. ''Why would she fear that anything would happen to me?''

''Bahanian law requires that a royal child be raised in the palace. I suspect Fiona feared that if I knew about you, I would insist you be raised here. If she didn't marry me, she would lose you.'' He sighed. ''I like to think I would not have insisted, but I don't know that it's true. After I lost her, I would have given anything to have a part of her with me.'' He touched her hand. ''And now you are here.''

Zara smiled tightly as she held on to her glass of cola. ''Yes, well, it's all very strange.''

''How did you find me now?''

Zara explained about the papers the lawyer had sent. ''Once I read the letters, I started to consider the impossible.''

''Zara insisted we take the tour,'' Cleo announced cheerfully. ''I wanted to walk up to the front door and knock. She said the guards wouldn't have let us in.''

The king smiled. ''Even one as charming as you, Cleo, might have had a little trouble getting past the royal guard. Although I suspect you have a way with men. I'll have to warn my sons about you.''

Cleo flicked her wrist. ''I've sworn off princes,

Your Highness. They're just all the same. Rich, powerful...it gets boring after a while."

Zara rose from her seat and crossed to the French doors leading to the balcony. Rafe came up behind her.

"Are you all right?" he asked.

She shook her head. "Would you be, under the circumstances?"

"Probably not."

"Everything is so confusing."

"There's nothing to be confused about," Hassan announced as he stood. "After twenty-eight years, my daughter has returned to me."

"You make it sound so simple and I can barely catch my breath."

Her father—she couldn't believe that was possible—nodded. "This is unfamiliar to us both. Perhaps we should take the time to acquaint ourselves with the situation. I wish to show you my world. Bahania is a country blessed with great resources and people. You must see the beauty of it. We will start with you and Cleo moving into the palace."

"All right!" Cleo clapped her hands together. "I think I'm going to like having you in the family," she told the king.

Zara wasn't so sure. "Our hotel is very comfortable," she said. Both Hassan and Cleo looked at her as if she were crazy.

"You are my daughter," Hassan reminded her. "As such, the palace is your home. You will be made to feel welcome. We will have time together."

"Your Highness, you need to think this through," Zara said. "I mean I know I look like your daughter and Fiona is my mother and you *did* have a relationship with her, but you have to be sure about this. Shouldn't we take blood tests?''

"I know what is right and I know who you are." He walked over to hug her. ''After so very many years, you are where you belong. That is all that matters. Come, you will collect your things and move into the palace right now.''

Zara glanced around, searching for an escape. Her gaze settled on Rafe. For some reason he seemed the only sane person in the room.

''Are you going to be there?'' she asked before she could stop herself. ''At the palace? Do you live there?''

Rafe nodded. ''For the next few weeks.''

Hassan stared at him. ''That's right. You *will* be at the palace. You have found my most beloved treasure and brought her to me. Therefore, I will entrust her to you.''

Zara slipped free of Hassan's embrace. ''I don't understand.''

Rafe looked as if he'd just sucked a lemon. ''Your Highness I don't—''

Hassan cut him off with a shake of his head. ''My mind is made up. I will only trust you with her safety. It will be a temporary matter, until you return to your regular duties.''

''Trust him for what?'' Zara asked.

''Rafe will be your bodyguard. He will protect you with his life.''

Chapter Four

Rafe held in a groan. He did *not* need this kind of trouble in his life. Protecting royalty wasn't that big a deal—he'd been in charge of Prince Kardal's security for three years. But guarding the king of Bahania's newly found, soon-to-be-favorite daughter wasn't his idea of a good time. Especially when the king had more in mind than her physical protection. King Hassan wouldn't want anyone messing with Zara for any reason—including and probably especially sex.

Which meant his physical attraction toward her could be a one-way to ticket to a headless moment, should he be foolish enough to let his libido overrule his common sense. Not that he would ever let that happen.

"Your Highness," he said, trying to figure out how to reason with the king without creating trouble.

Hassan waved away his concerns before he could even voice them. "As a temporary measure, Rafe. I'm not unmindful of your duties to my son-in-law."

Zara glanced between them, obviously confused. "What are you two talking about?"

Cleo bounced off the sofa and fluffed her short blond hair. "What your new father is saying is that Rafe has been assigned to protect you with his very life. While I could be taken by terrorists and tortured, and everyone would just yawn."

Hassan smiled at her. "Rafe will keep you under his care, as well," he said. "While you are my guest, your safety is of equal concern. You are the most-beloved sister of the daughter of my heart's desire."

"Could I get that on a plaque?" Cleo asked.

"Perhaps a tapestry," the king told her. "We could have the weaving women design one."

"You have weaving women?" Cleo sounded horrified. "Is that what they do with their entire day? Weave? Do you…" Her voice trailed off as she caught the king's smile. "You're teasing me."

"Yes."

Cleo shrugged. "He's got a sense of humor. Who knew?"

Zara didn't respond. She still looked as if she was in shock. Hassan hugged her one last time.

"I leave you in the protection of your bodyguard. Rafe will make all the arrangements to move you into the palace. I look forward to seeing you there."

With that, he was gone. Cleo shook her head. "This is amazing. Just like in a movie."

Rafe wished it was a movie. Then he could get out of his seat and head back to his regular life. Instead he was stuck. He supposed that he could go to his boss and complain, but that would annoy King Hassan.

Zara folded her arms over her chest. "He can't be serious. He wants you to be my bodyguard?"

"I'm more than qualified."

She opened her mouth, then closed it. "This isn't about your abilities, Rafe. It's about being sane. Who on earth would want to hurt me? No one knows who I am."

"You might be Hassan's daughter. I know it sounds far-fetched, but go along with it for now, all right? This is a temporary situation."

"Don't you have a real job you'd rather be doing?"

He was supposed to be coordinating the development of an air force in Bahania, El Bahar and the City of Thieves. "That is going to have to wait for a while."

Prince Kardal, his boss, would understand. At this point in the negotiations no one wanted to annoy King Hassan. Which meant Rafe would spend the next few weeks making sure Zara didn't get so much as a splinter. It would mean long hours and close contact with the first woman to get his attention in years. Life had a hell of a sense of humor.

"Look at the bright side," Cleo said. "At least the

king didn't throw you out on your butt. If anything, he seemed really happy to see you.''

Zara nodded. ''I don't know what to think about any of this. I guess we should head back to the hotel and pack up our stuff.''

Cleo did a couple of quick dance steps. ''I'm gonna live in a palace,'' she sang as she shimmied around the sofa. ''And you wanted to go camping in Yellowstone instead of coming here.''

Zara headed for the door. ''I'm beginning to think that would have been a better idea.''

''I don't have any experience with this whole bodyguard thing,'' Zara said as Rafe followed them back to their hotel. ''Do you plan to go with me everywhere?''

''Pretty much.''

''Will you carry the groceries when we go to the supermarket?'' Cleo asked.

''You won't be doing grocery shopping,'' Rafe told her.

Zara was still focused on the whole ''go with her everywhere'' concept. ''I don't have a very interesting life,'' she admitted. ''You're going to get bored.''

''I'll manage.''

They crossed the street and walked toward the entrance to the hotel where she and Cleo had stayed. Was this tall, dangerous man really going to shadow her, day and night? Was it possible?

''You know, you could just meet us at the palace,'' she said. ''We can take a cab.''

He didn't bother answering.

A bodyguard? It was too weird to believe. Of course there was a chance that King Hassan might be her father, which put the whole bodyguard dilemma in perspective. Her life had suddenly taken on the unreal qualities of a visit to a fun house.

Zara had seen some physical similarities between herself and the king, but she hadn't felt any kind of emotional connection. *He'd* been so sure and *she'd* wanted to head for home. It was one thing to be ten years old and long for a father to sweep into her life and give her the stability she'd always wanted. It was another to be grown-up, with a life of her own and find out she might be related to a ruling monarch.

When they reached the hotel, Rafe escorted them to their room. Once there, he actually checked the small space before allowing them to enter.

"Because terrorists might want to kidnap me?" she asked, slightly bemused as he stepped aside to let them in.

"Because I'm good at what I do."

His blue eyes were just as cold as they'd always been, but now she found them less scary. Perhaps because he was her only link to sanity in this impossible situation.

Cleo headed into the hotel room. Rafe briefly touched Zara's arm to detain her.

"I'm going to make some phone calls while you pack," he said, pulling a cell phone from his coat pocket. "Don't let anyone in the room but me."

"Is there a code word?" she asked.

"Troublemaker."

"I like that. I've always been a good girl."

"It's my job to make sure that doesn't change."

"Don't tell Cleo. She's *always* getting in trouble."

"Cleo isn't my concern."

"Figures." Zara glanced down the hall to make sure they were alone, then lowered her voice. "What if I don't want to go live at the palace?"

"If you're Hassan's daughter, that's where you belong."

She asked him because there was no one else. And because she trusted him to tell her the truth. "If I am, it's going to change everything, isn't it?"

He didn't answer. For several heartbeats they simply stared at each other. Zara became aware of a heat generated by the powerful man in front of her. Despite the strange situations she'd encountered in the past few hours, Rafe was a haven of safety. Which made no sense—the man had pulled a gun on her that morning.

She had the most ridiculous urge to cuddle up next to him, to feel his strong body pressing against hers as his arms held her close. She wanted to hear the steady beat of his heart. She wanted him to—

"You'd better get your packing done," he said. "I'll have a car here in twenty minutes."

Zara stepped into the room. Obviously, she was the only one having any kind of fantasies. It was a little disheartening, but not a big surprise. Men had never been very interested in her that way. Maybe it was the glasses.

She pushed at the wire frames as she moved toward her suitcase tucked in a corner of the room.

"Isn't this incredible?" Cleo asked as she came out

of the bathroom, her arms filled with cosmetics. "We are going to be in a palace. I can't believe it. I bet our rooms are amazing. Just that little bit we saw on the tour was fabulous, and those were the places where they allow the public. It's probably even better in the private quarters. Zara? What's wrong? You don't look excited."

"I'm in shock. All of this is happening too fast."

"Yeah, but it's great."

Zara wanted to say that she didn't agree, but she knew Cleo wouldn't understand. To her sister the situation was simple. The king of Bahania might be Zara's father—let's have a party. Zara was more concerned with the reality of trying to fit in to that kind of a world. While she and her mother had never starved, they'd certainly never had a lot of money. Her idea of a luxurious vacation was one where she didn't have to cook.

"I'll deal with it later," she told herself as she packed her clothes and put her toiletries into a carry-on bag.

When Rafe knocked on the door ten minutes later, they were ready to go.

"We can carry these down ourselves," Zara said as he entered the room.

Instead of responding, he opened the door wider. Two men entered and picked up their heavy suitcases as if they were empty soda cans. Cleo looked at her and shrugged.

"Okay," her sister said. "So the rich and royal live different. I can adjust!"

Zara followed her to the elevator and wasn't the

least bit surprised when they walked outside and found a limo waiting.

"Because a car isn't good enough?" she asked, sliding into the back seat.

"I didn't know how much luggage you'd have," Rafe told her.

The two men finished with their bags and slammed the trunk. As they walked toward the front of the vehicle, one of them slipped off his jacket. Zara saw a shoulder holster as he shifted onto the front seat. She glared at Rafe who sat across from them.

"They're armed?"

"Standard precaution."

Not in her world. The small college town where she lived and worked barely required her to remember to pull the key out of her car ignition.

"Try not to think about it," he said. "Once you're within the walls of the palace, you won't have to worry about any of that. You're safe, and I'll be close by."

How close? she wanted to ask but didn't. Somehow those words took on a whole new meaning where Rafe was concerned. Instead she glanced at her watch and realized that a mere eight hours ago she and Cleo had been eating breakfast in their hotel. Who knew a world could change so quickly?

"Tell me about the royal family," she said to distract herself. "What are they going to think about me?"

"I doubt they'll be too surprised. Hassan is known as a man who likes women."

"Are there other illegitimate children?"

"Not that I'm aware of."

He looked comfortable in his leather seat. That morning he'd been dressed like a desert nomad. Now he wore a suit, but he was trusted with her safety.

"Are *you* armed?" she asked.

"You have plenty of other things to worry about," he told her.

She took that as a yes.

Cleo rubbed the soft seat. "There are princes, right? Four of them?"

Rafe nodded.

"Any of them married?"

"Cleo!" Zara glared at her sister. "We're not here to make trouble."

"I'm not interested in trouble. I've given up on men, remember. I just thought this is my one opportunity to meet a real prince instead of just reading about them in magazines." She returned her attention to Rafe. "Are they young and good-looking?"

"They're in their late twenties and early thirties," he said. "I'm not in a position to comment on their appearance."

"I suppose if one is a wealthy prince, appearance isn't all that important."

Zara eyed her sister's short blond hair and curvy figure. "They're going to love you," she said mournfully. "Try not to complicate the situation."

"I swear." Cleo made an X over her heart.

Zara wasn't impressed. Cleo might not go looking for trouble, but it could very well come looking for her. After all, Cleo attracted men the way magnets drew metal. She'd had her first date sometime in her first year of high school and had rarely been without a boyfriend—until recently, Zara reminded herself. Cleo had sworn off men a few months before. She wondered if that resolution would withstand the prince test.

They drove through the streets of the city. Traffic slowed their progress, and Zara had the urge to jump out and get lost in the crowd. With her luck she would trip and break something important.

"King Hassan isn't married now, is he?" she asked.

"He's between wives," Rafe answered.

"I thought so. I did some research on the Internet. I remember reading that there are four princes, plus Princess Sabra." She frowned. "The king says she goes by Sabrina, right?"

"Yes. What else did you learn?"

"Just about everything," Cleo said, interrupting. "Zara is the queen of research. She could tell you the top three exports of Bahania, the gross national product and a lot of other boring facts designed to put a room of insomniacs to sleep."

Zara ignored her. "I'm a college professor. Research is a big part of that."

"What's your subject?" he asked.

Cleo leaned forward. "Women's studies. Our little princess-to-be is something of a feminist."

Rafe winced.

"I'm not rabid about it," Zara protested. "To change the subject to something more relevant—you need to persuade the king to agree to a blood test. We have to be sure that I'm his daughter."

"I think it's a little late for you to back out now," he said.

Cleo gave a long-suffering sigh. "You've wanted this all your life. I can't believe you're questioning your good fortune."

"Thinking about finding my father and actually finding him are two different things."

The limo turned onto a private drive and passed between two large gates. Up ahead through the trees she could catch glimpses of the famed pink palace—home of the Bahanian royal family.

"Really different," she breathed as the panic seeped in.

There were servants in the palace. Servants and guards and priceless treasures. All of this had probably been discussed on the tour, but Zara had been too nervous to pay attention. Of course anyone thinking about a palace would assume such things existed, but she hadn't been thinking, either. At least not sensibly. So here she was, being led down a long corridor, led by *servants* and passing *guards*. It was enough to give a healthy person a heart attack.

Even the normally bubbly Cleo was subdued as they walked and walked, passing huge rooms filled with Western-style furniture and open areas with pillows and cushions instead of chairs and sofas. There were statues and fountains and tapestries and cats. Many, many cats.

Zara had heard about Hassan's love of felines, but she hadn't realized they had their run of the palace.

At least the cats were clean and well behaved, she thought as one approached and sniffed the luggage.

Finally their party stopped in front of a large door in a corridor of many doors. The head servant of their group—an attractive woman in her late forties—opened the door and motioned for them to step inside. Zara turned to Rafe and impulsively gripped his arm.

"Are you going to be close by?"

She managed to get out the sentence before her body registered the heat of him radiating through his suit jacket sleeve. Her bones started to feel that melting sensation again, which was almost more than she could stand. It wasn't enough that she was entering a world as unfamiliar to her as another planet. No, she also had to be incredibly sexually attracted to a man for the first time in her life.

Rafe's blue eyes stared into hers. She prayed that he couldn't know how she was reacting to him. His pity, not to mention the rejection, would be more than she could handle today.

"You're my responsibility," he told her. "I'll be around and you'll be fine."

"What if I'm not?"

He smiled. A warm, friendly sort of smile that made her muscles quiver—because the bone melting wasn't bad enough. Then he gently pushed her toward the door.

"Go on," he said. "You might like it."

"Liar."

But there was no turning back. She drew in a deep breath and prepared to enter a new world.

They had not been assigned a room—instead there

was a suite at their disposal. Zara's first impression
was of space and beauty. Cream-colored walls soared
up at least fifteen feet. Opposite the door, floor-to-
ceiling windows and glass doors allowed a view of
the deep blue Arabian Sea beyond the large balcony.
She had the brief thought that the water was the same
color as Rafe's eyes, then she told herself not to go
there—it would only be dangerous and potentially humiliating.

Two sofas and several chairs formed a conversation
group around a large square table made of inlaid
wood. Large pillows were piled up in the corners of
the room. Tapestries in deep blues and rose covered
the pale walls, and underfoot an intricate tile pattern
formed a maze.

''You each have a bedroom,'' the woman said, mo-
tioning to identical doors on either side of the vast
living room. ''His Highness thought you would prefer
to be together, but if you would rather have separate
quarters, that can be arranged.''

She looked at Zara as she spoke. Zara glanced at
Cleo, who shrugged.

''This is fine,'' Zara told the woman. ''The room
is lovely.''

''If you will tell me which luggage goes in which
room?''

Zara pointed to her two suitcases. A different servant took them to the left. Cleo's were taken to the
right. Zara trailed after her bags and found herself in
a massive bedroom.

A four-poster bed stood in the center of the room.
Two steps led up to the high mattress. Double doors

led to the same balcony she'd seen from the main room. An oversize armoire held a television and DVD unit. Drawers below offered a selection of American and foreign movies.

Dazed and with her senses on overload, Zara moved into the bathroom where she nearly fainted with delight. A private walled garden grew at the edge of the tub. Sunlight dappled the tile floor, illuminating a long vanity and double sinks. The shower could easily hold five or six people, and there were baskets of shampoo, lotion and soaps, all from expensive boutiques. It was girl heaven.

Zara turned and saw the head servant waiting expectantly. "It's beautiful," she told her. "Everything is lovely."

The woman smiled. "I will tell the king you are pleased. Would you like us to unpack for you?"

Zara thought about her discount clothes and the ratty state of some of her underwear. "Um, no. Thanks. We can manage."

The woman bowed and left, taking the other servants with her. It was only then that she realized Rafe hadn't followed her into her room. Where was he staying? Not that she needed to concern herself with the arrangements. No doubt the palace had plenty of room for her temporary bodyguard.

"Can you believe it?" Cleo asked.

Zara stepped into the living room. "What's your room like?"

"Come see. It's amazing. It's something out of a movie or a dream."

Cleo's room was identical to Zara's, right down to

the baskets of soaps and lotions. Cleo climbed the two steps and threw herself on her bed.

"I'm never going home. This is fabulous. When I grow up, I want to be the daughter of a king, too."

Zara laughed at her sister's pleasure. "Wait until you see the harem."

Cleo sat up, her eyes wide. "There's a harem?"

Zara held up her hands. "I don't know. I was kidding. I didn't read anything about it. I have no idea how old the palace is, but it's possible."

"I'm going to ask the king the next time I see him." Cleo flung herself back on the mattress. "I can't believe I'm saying that. The next time I see the king. How did you get so lucky?"

Zara didn't answer. While she, too, was overwhelmed by the luxury of the suite, she still felt uneasy about being in the palace. Everything was so unfamiliar. At least she and Cleo had each other.

A knock on the door drew her into the living room. She found herself hoping it was Rafe, checking up on her. Her heart beat faster at the thought, but when she pulled open the door, the person waiting in the hall was a woman.

Zara opened her mouth to say hello but had to close it without speaking. All rational thought fled. Her mind filled with thoughts, went blank, then exploded with questions.

The woman standing in front of her looked to be about her age. They were of similar height, although Zara was a couple of inches taller. But it was her face that captured Zara's attention. The shape of the eyes and the mouth. The angle of the cheekbones. The similarities were striking, although the mystery woman was far more attractive. Zara's stomach plunged for her toes.

"You must be Zara," the young woman said. "I see what my father meant when he said we could almost be twins. At the very least, it's obvious we're sisters."

They both had dark hair. Zara nervously pushed up her glasses. "So you must be Princess Sabra?"

The woman nodded. "Call me Sabrina." She slipped past Zara and stepped into the suite. "Nice room. I heard you have a sister, but she's not really your sister? Is that right?"

"I'm Cleo."

Sabrina turned toward the voice, saw Cleo entering the living room and smiled. "Well, we don't look anything alike. Is your hair really that color? It's gorgeous."

Cleo fingered her spiky blond hair. "This is me. I tried being a redhead for a while, but blond roots look really weird, let me tell you."

Zara closed the door. She didn't know what to think or say. This was her half sister. Princess Sabra...aka Sabrina. She was stunning in her elegant clothes. She wore slacks and a silk blouse that looked expensive. Zara fingered her own bargain cotton dress. Geometric gold earrings caught the light and there was a huge diamond on Sabrina's left ring finger. She moved with an elegant grace that reminded Zara of her mother. Fiona had been forever trying to teach her to *glide* rather than stomp, but Zara had never learned the lesson.

The three of them stood awkwardly in the center of the room. Zara couldn't escape the feeling of being a bad copy of a stunning original. As usual Cleo broke the ice.

"So what do we call you?" Cleo asked. "Your Highness?"

"Just Sabrina."

"And you're really a princess?"

"From the day I was born." Sabrina moved to one of the sofas and motioned for them to join her.

"You sound American," Cleo said, sitting at the opposite end of the same sofa. "The king has a bit of a Middle-Eastern accent."

"I spent a lot of my life in California. I can, like, do the Valley Girl thing if it makes you more comfortable."

Cleo grinned. "Cool. So you live here, now?"

"I live close by."

Cleo pointed at her diamond. "Great ring."

"Thank you."

"Is there a husband to go along with that?"

"Absolutely. Prince Kardal. We've been married about a year."

"A prince and princess. Just like in the fairy tales." Cleo sighed. "I can't believe we're here. This is so not our regular life."

Sabrina turned her dark gaze on Zara. "Where are you from?"

"Washington State. It's in the northwest part of the country."

"Zara's a professor," Cleo confided. "She's really

smart. I live about eighty miles away in Spokane where I manage a copy shop.''

''And now you're in Bahania,'' Sabrina said. The words sounded welcoming enough, but there was an edge to her tone that made Zara uncomfortable.

Did Sabrina resent her being there? Dumb question, she thought. She was a complete stranger who arrived from nowhere with a preposterous story about being King Hassan's illegitimate daughter.

''I know this is unexpected,'' Zara said quietly. ''For all of us. I don't know how much the king told you about why I'm here and all.''

''He mentioned that you had recently found some letters he had sent to your mother. Apparently theirs was a great love affair.''

Sabrina smiled, but there wasn't any humor in her eyes. Zara folded her arms over her chest. She felt awkward and unwelcome. Sabrina was everything she herself was not—elegant, beautiful, well dressed. Zara was reminded of all the times she'd attended her mother's dance classes and hadn't been able to help tripping over her own feet. Eventually Fiona had given up trying to teach her daughter to be graceful.

''What I don't understand is how the two of you ever became sisters,'' Sabrina said.

Cleo shrugged. ''It was just one of those things.'' She began telling the story.

Zara listened for a few minutes, then quietly rose and headed for the French doors. Maybe a few minutes outside would clear her head...or at least help her feel more as if she belonged here. Not that she did.

She stepped out onto the balcony and caught her breath. The city stretched out on either side of the palace. She could see a few buildings over the tree-tops of the lush gardens surrounding the royal lands. More impressive than that was her view of the ocean. She walked to the railing and leaned against the warm metal. The soft, heavy air covered her in a hot blanket. She could smell exotic flowers and a faint scent of the ocean beyond. She'd never seen anything so lovely.

And yet she desperately wanted to go home. How stupid was that? She was on the verge of having every fantasy ever come true and her heart's desire was to bolt for safety. She was a coward—or an idiot. Maybe both.

She closed her eyes and let the heat seep into her. The sun had moved low toward the horizon. It was nearly sunset. She felt as if she'd traveled a thousand miles in just one day.

She heard a sound behind her. Before she could turn, she heard a familiar voice that sent shivers dancing along her spine.

"Want to talk about it?"

Chapter Five

Zara turned and found Rafe lounging in the doorway to the room next to hers. On cue, her bones began their slow dissolve and her heart performed a steady but disconcerting cha-cha. He'd removed his jacket and loosened his tie. What was it about a man in semidisarray that sent the most sensible woman on the planet into emotional regression?

"Are we neighbors?" she asked, doing her darnedest to keep her voice from coming out in a squeak.

"As your temporary bodyguard it's necessary for me to stay close."

Was it her imagination or did his voice sound more like a purr? Or maybe she was being affected by all the cats in the palace.

"I'm sorry they made you move quarters."

He shrugged. "It's no big deal. Are you getting settled?"

"Some. The suite is huge. I think the bathroom has more square feet than my town house back home. Everything is lovely."

She turned back to face the water. When Rafe joined her at the balcony, she told herself not to read too much into his actions. A man like him would never be interested in a woman like her. If all the disasters that made up her personal life weren't enough to remind her of her unfortunate past, there was always Jon.

"You don't sound very excited," Rafe said. "Having second thoughts?"

"Try five hundredth thoughts."

"You came looking for your father for a reason. You must have wanted to find him."

"I did. I know it's not logical to be questioning everything now. I should shut up and be grateful."

"Maybe. At least he was happy to see you."

She nodded. "Too happy. His reaction is all about Fiona. He doesn't know me, yet." She pointed to the water. "Look at where we're standing. How is this possible?"

"The palace occupies some great real estate. At least your father isn't a used-camel dealer."

Despite her confusion and Rafe's nearness, she smiled. "I don't believe there is such a thing."

Rafe looked at her and smiled slightly. "Sure there is. The aftermarket for camels is a booming business."

The sight of his smile turned her heart's cha-cha

into a tango. A tiny quivering need took up residence in her stomach. For reasons she didn't understand, something about this man got to her on a very primitive level. She would have to remember to try not to drool in front of him.

"What do you do here?" she asked. "You're an American. How did you get to Bahania?"

"Same way as you. By plane." He straightened and leaned one narrow hip against the railing. "Actually I work for Princess Sabrina's husband—Prince Kardal. I'm a security and tactical expert."

"That doesn't tell me much."

"You'd find my work very boring."

She doubted that, but decided not to press. There might be a very good reason Rafe was being reticent. At this point she hardly needed *more* information. She was already too close to overload.

"I've met Princess Sabrina," she said. "She's inside making friends with Cleo."

"Your sister is very friendly."

That was hardly news. "I know. I'm the smart one. She's the funny, sexy, adorable one. At least she can distract all the family members so they don't notice me."

"Oh, they'll notice."

She shook her head. "If you're trying to make me feel better, you're doing a lousy job. I hate meeting a lot of people at once. I can never get the names straight and I doubt the royal family will consent to wear name tags."

"Probably not. But there are compensations. Look at the palace."

"I'm not in it for the money."

"I almost believe you."

He spoke so lightly that at first she thought he was kidding, but when she glanced at him, she saw the truth in his blue eyes.

"I thought we'd covered this material," she told him. "You all but accused me of wanting to blackmail the king. After you checked me out, I thought you'd changed your mind."

"I'm 98 percent convinced."

"Tell me when you are 100 percent."

"I will."

She straightened and walked toward a bench between the doors to their rooms. "Is that what everyone is going to be thinking?" she asked as she sat down. "That I'm some horrible person out for what I can get?"

"The king doesn't think that and his is the only opinion that matters."

Zara wasn't so sure about that. She found herself caring about Rafe's good opinion. Of course that was more about her hormones than anything else.

"At least this situation puts the rest of my life in perspective," she said.

"Just think about the excitement of being a princess."

Princess? She hadn't thought that part of it through. "No," she said without thinking. "That's not possible."

Cleo would jump at the chance, but then, her sister had more of a princess personality. Zara rubbed her temples as she held in a groan. Cleo was the charming one. She could talk to anyone and men adored her. She, Zara, was painfully shy, awkward with strangers and had a horrible track record with men. In the past couple of years she'd begun to think there was something seriously wrong with her.

"Zara?"

She looked up and saw that Rafe had settled on the far end of the bench. She angled toward him. "This will never work. I'm hardly princess material. I barely know anything about Bahania, either the country or the customs. I'm sure to put a foot wrong. I'm not sophisticated or pretty. I'm a college professor from a small town no one has heard of. My idea of an exciting Friday night is going to a basketball game by myself. I can't even get a date. My God, if everyone thought I was a freak before because I was a virgin, what are they going to think now?"

Her words hung in the late-afternoon heat. Zara blinked several times, hoping she hadn't actually said her thoughts aloud. Unfortunately, the stunned expression on Rafe's face told her that she had.

Humiliation washed over her. She felt her cheeks flame and started to get to her feet.

"Forget I said that," she mumbled, just as his hand settled on her forearm.

"Don't even think about going anywhere."

She sank back on her seat and ducked her head. "I didn't mean it."

"Which part?"

"All of it."

"There you are."

Zara looked up, grateful for the interruption. Sabrina had stepped out onto the balcony. Rafe rose to his feet. Sabrina shot him a look.

"Oh, please," she said with a laugh. "You're going all formal on me *now?*"

"We're in a different place."

Sabrina sighed, her smile fading. "Tell me about it." She turned her attention to Zara, who also stood. "I wanted to let you know that you and Cleo have been invited to a formal dinner tomorrow night. My father is entertaining several visiting dignitaries. My brothers will be there, as well. It's a good opportunity for you to meet the family."

The world began to spin. Zara tried to breathe but couldn't. "A f-formal dinner?" she stuttered. "I don't think that's such a good idea."

"Sorry. The king insists." Sabrina didn't look all that sorry. "Don't worry. You won't be expected to do much more than show up and chat with some of the guests."

"But my presence isn't appropriate. We don't even know for sure that I'm his daughter."

"The king specifically said he wants you and Cleo there. If you plan not to attend, I suggest you take it up with him."

"Not a good idea," Rafe said quickly, as if he really thought she might complain to King Hassan that she didn't want to accept his invitation. Not that she did, but she wasn't about to share the fact publicly.

Even though she was standing outdoors, she felt walls closing in around her. "I, ah, don't have anything to wear." Or the ability to pay for a dress that nice. Still, that was why they'd invented credit cards. She'd have to deal with the blow to her budget later. "Is there a store nearby where Cleo and I can shop?"

Sabrina sighed. "I could loan you something." She looked Zara up and down. "You're taller and thinner, which is a little annoying, but I think I can recover. I'll see what I can find."

Zara couldn't tell if the princess was kidding or not. She had a bad feeling that Sabrina didn't like her, although she didn't know why. She wouldn't have thought she'd been in town long enough to annoy anyone.

"You're very kind," Zara said, trying to sound gracious.

"Whatever." Sabrina turned to leave, then paused. "Although there won't be an official announcement about who you are, people are bound to notice the likeness. So be prepared to be the center of attention. No one will be rude enough to ask outright, but they will hint."

With that, she gave a smile and headed back into Zara's room. Zara sank back on the bench.

"Why does she hate me?"

She expected Rafe to deny any such emotion. When he didn't say anything right away, she glanced at him. He'd shoved his hands into his pockets and looked almost uncomfortable with the question.

"She doesn't hate you...exactly."

Zara closed her eyes. "What does that mean?"

"It's a long story."

"I don't seem to have any formal engagements until tomorrow."

Rafe settled next to her again. "Sabrina's parents married in haste, as they say. By the time she came along, there was already trouble in the relationship. They divorced fairly quickly, and when her mother asked permission for her to be taken out of Bahania, the king agreed. Sabrina was raised spending the school year with her mother in California and her summers here."

Zara shook her head. "Wait a minute. What do you mean 'her mother asked permission to take her out of the country'?"

"Bahanian law requires that royal children be raised within the borders of the country. It's not that uncommon. El Bahar has similar requirements. While royal couples can divorce, they can't take their children away. That way the monarchy ensures that the heirs are raised knowing about their country and their people."

Zara thought that made sense, although it was difficult to relate to. "So Sabrina was a child of both countries. Why is that bad?"

"No prince or princess had been allowed to leave before. In essence, Hassan didn't care enough about his daughter to keep her around."

Zara didn't like the sound of that. "Maybe he did care. Maybe her mother loved her so much that—"

Rafe cut her off with a shake of his head. "Neither of Sabrina's parents were very interested in her. She was shuttled back and forth all her life, left in the care of nannies and maids. Sabrina's an intelligent woman. She was an excellent student, but neither of her parents noticed. Because her mother lived something of a wild life, the press assumed the same about Sabrina, even though it wasn't true. Then her father arranged a marriage for her without consulting her. For her it was the last straw.''

''What happened?''

He hesitated. ''She ran away. It turned out well in the end. She married Prince Kardal and they're very happy together. However she and her father have only recently reconciled.''

Zara got it right away. ''So after twenty-plus years, they're finally starting to connect, but she's still bitter about all the years before. I show up out of nowhere and he welcomes me with open arms.''

''Exactly.''

Zara leaned back into the bench and groaned. ''I've been in the palace less than three hours and I already have an enemy. What's going to be next?''

Rafe found Prince Kardal in the security briefing room going over plans.

''Do you know how expensive the planes are going to be?'' the prince asked when he entered.

''Yes.'' Rafe slid into the seat across from his boss.

Like most modern rulers, Prince Kardal wore a suit rather than traditional garments. When he was home with his own people, he frequently returned to the old ways, but not while visiting a head of state—and his father-in-law.

Kardal, a tall, dark-haired man, tossed the plans to the table. ''Technology isn't cheap. I miss the old days, when we could patrol our country on camels.''

Rafe laughed. "Kardal, you're barely in your thirties. You're too young to remember those days."

The prince grinned. "Perhaps." He stretched. "I know why you have come to see me."

"I bet. You heard about Zara?"

"Is that her name?"

"Yes. Zara Paxton. She's a college professor from the Pacific Northwest. Some small town near Idaho."

Kardal raised his eyebrows. "Is it true? Is she Hassan's daughter?"

"Maybe." He shook his head. "Probably. The king needs to be sure, which means blood tests. But right now he's too excited to think logically. You know how he gets."

Kardal reached under his shirt cuff and touched the thick, gold slave bracelet there. "Yes, I know. Has Sabrina met with her?"

Rafe nodded. "She came by Zara's room about an hour ago."

"She cannot be happy about her father's enthusiasm."

"No." Which brought Rafe to another awkward point. "He's asked me to watch over Zara. Be a temporary bodyguard."

Kardal didn't say anything for a long time. Then the corners of his mouth turned up and he laughed.

Rafe shifted uncomfortably in his seat. "Yeah, it's a real knee-slapper. Thanks for the support."

Kardal didn't bother to apologize. He laughed a little longer, then finally spoke. "What is she like, this college professor?"

"Scared." He thought of Zara's pretty face and the

questions in her eyes. "She's overwhelmed by all that has happened. I don't think she was expecting to be moved into the palace so quickly."

Zara was as prepared to handle this as a rabbit was prepared to take on a pack of wolves. If she wasn't careful she was going to be eaten alive. He couldn't believe he was actually worried about her, but he was, dammit. What was wrong with him? He wasn't a good person. He didn't have altruistic feelings.

"Do you like her?" Kardal asked.

"I don't know her."

"You know what I mean."

Rafe did know. His boss wanted to know what Rafe felt in his gut. Was she someone to be trusted?

"She's all right," he said grudgingly.

"Such high praise will turn her head," Kardal teased. "So the king has requested you guard the treasure that is his daughter. We have at least three weeks until we return to the City of Thieves. I believe I can spare you, if you wish to honor the king's request."

"We both know it wasn't a request," Rafe grumbled.

"You are not his to command. You may certainly tell him no."

"I don't think so."

"You tell *me* no constantly."

"That's different. You can be reasoned with. Hassan isn't acting like a king, he's acting like a father. I don't want to annoy him just as we're setting up the joint air force."

The corners of Kardal's mouth twitched again. "So

the mighty hunter will be forced to guard a mere woman. However will your pride survive?''

Rafe wasn't all that worried about his pride. He'd had worse duty in his life. What made him nervous was his attraction to Zara. She'd reminded him of what it was like to want a woman. Only this woman was completely off-limits. Not only was she under his protection, she was the king's daughter and a virgin. He still couldn't believe she'd blurted out that particular fact, but saw no reason why she would lie. Which meant she was telling the truth. Which also meant if he wanted to keep his head firmly on his shoulders, he was going to have to keep his pants zipped and his mind on business.

Zara awakened sometime after midnight. She was impressed that she'd been able to sleep at all what with all the strange thoughts and images zooming through her brain. As she opened her eyes, she half expected to find herself back in her modest hotel room—or even in her bedroom in Washington State. As if this entire experience had been a dream. But instead, she found herself staring at unfamiliar yet luxurious furnishings.

She was really here—really in the Bahanian royal palace after meeting the man who could be her father—probably *was* her father. A thousand questions filled her brain. Realizing that sleep was now impossible, she collected her robe and glasses, then climbed out of her bed. She crossed to the French doors leading out to the balcony and stepped into the darkness.

She was instantly assaulted by the scent of the garden and the faint fragrance of the sea. Brine added an edge to the sweetness of hundreds of flowers that were little more than blurs in the starlight. A soft, warm breeze made her pull her robe more tightly around her body.

She raised her head, staring at the sky. The stars seemed different. Her memories of her lone astronomy class had faded to the point where she couldn't remember if being halfway around the world meant she really *was* seeing different stars. If she were in a different hemisphere, there were different stars. She recalled that much. But here in Bahania—

"You're looking serious about something."

Rafe's voice came out of the darkness by his room. Zara supposed she should have been shocked, or even afraid. Instead she found herself eager for his company. She took a step toward where she guessed he was standing, then remembered it was the middle of the night and she wasn't dressed to receive visitors.

"I was trying to figure out if these are the same stars I see when I'm home," she said.

"Some would be, although they'd rise and set at different times."

He stepped toward her, just close enough for a shaft of light from a nearby window to fall on him. She saw that he'd changed into jeans and a T-shirt. His short blond hair looked faintly mussed, as if he'd been asleep. His feet were bare. The realization made her own toes curl slightly at the implied intimacy. They'd both been asleep. She wore a nightgown and robe. Underneath, she had on panties and nothing else. Despite the layers of her clothing, she felt exposed and extremely aware of him as a man.

A sensible woman would have ducked back into her room. Zara knew that she was naturally sensible, that her sister was not, and most of the time Cleo had way more fun. Maybe it was time to see how the other half lived.

She took a single step toward Rafe. "I couldn't sleep. I guess it's all the excitement."

"That makes sense. It's been less than twenty-four hours and your entire world is different."

Had it only been a single day? She felt that she'd known him much longer.

He motioned to the bench they'd shared before. "Come on. I'll tell you a bedtime story."

The low intimacy of his voice sent shivers up her spine. Rafe wasn't like anyone she'd ever met. He was strong and took charge: very different from the academic sort she was used to.

She moved to the bench and sat. Rafe settled next to her, not crowding her, but sitting close enough for her to be incredibly aware of him. He breathed deeply, each inhale filling his chest. In the semidarkness, his blue eyes looked more black...and bottomless. She studied the shape of his strong jaw and the way the stubble growing there emphasized the hollows and planes of his features.

He shifted slightly, causing muscles to ripple. She thought about the feel of his body on hers when he'd attacked her and the way he'd held a gun to her head.

"Who are you?" she asked. "Earlier today you were dressed in traditional garments, yet you had a gun and were in the palace. You know the king well enough to get in to see him just by asking. You're an American, yet you're obviously comfortable in this foreign country.''

He shrugged. ''I'm just a guy doing his job. Currently that means keeping you safe.''

''You know what I mean, Rafe.''

''Yeah, I know, but I'm not going to tell you.''

''I'm a good security risk.''

He turned to face her, his dark eyes lasering into hers. ''I don't know that yet. Until I'm sure, I won't be spilling any state secrets.''

His intensity made her squirm. ''Do you know any?'' she asked lightly.

His teeth flashed as he smiled. ''Just the one about turning straw into gold.''

''That's an important one.''

He briefly touched her shoulder. ''Don't take it personally,'' he said. ''If you stick around long enough, you'll find out who I am and what I do. For now it's enough that you know that I usually work for Sabrina's husband.''

She'd felt the pressure of his fingertips all the way down to her fingers. A distinct tingling there made her want to make a fist.

''Can you talk about what you did before that?''

He leaned back into the bench. ''I spent a few years with a private paramilitary organization. They contracted with the government, taking care of things that couldn't be legally sanctioned.''

She blinked. ''Things like what?''

His smile faded. ''Let your imagination run wild.

Small wars, finding terrorists, preventing kidnappings.''

He spoke matter-of-factly. As if he'd simply helped a group of kids to cross the street. Zara knew it was much more than that. Whatever he'd done had been dangerous and scary—a far cry from her quiet, academic life.

''And before that?'' she asked.

''I was in the army. I went to college on an ROTC scholarship, then I spent ten years serving my country.''

She glanced at his short hair and his straight posture. She could imagine him in uniform, leading troops into battle. No doubt he'd been cool under fire.

''It's a long way from the military to the wilds of Bahania,'' she murmured. ''Do you miss it?''

''The States or the army?''

''Either. Both.''

''Sometimes. I was too much of a rebel to advance much more in my career. I got out while everyone thought I was a hero. As for missing the States, there are places I'd like to see again. I don't have an actual home I long for. I've always been one to move around.''

That sounded familiar. She'd lost track of the number of times Fiona had made them move. ''What about family?'' she asked.

Nothing about Rafe changed, yet she would have sworn that an invisible wall came down between them.

''No family,'' he said easily.

He had to have some kind of family somewhere.

He hadn't just hatched under a rock. But her years with Cleo had taught her that there were some things people didn't want to talk about.

Was he married?

The question appeared in her brain, but she couldn't force the words out. They implied an interest, which, while it might be true, made her uncomfortable.

"Any kids?" she asked instead.

Rafe shifted so that he angled toward her, placing one arm along the back of the bench. His fingers were millimeters from her shoulder. She almost couldn't breathe.

"I'm not married, Zara."

The statement danced against her spine like hot water sizzling on a stove. She felt herself blushing, then figured it was dark enough that it didn't matter. He wouldn't be able to tell. Or maybe he would, she thought, glancing at him and quickly looking away when she caught him staring. He was the kind of man who just might notice everything about a woman.

"I didn't ask about a wife," she clarified, as if he would be fooled.

"Of course not." He flashed her another smile. "So tell me about your life before becoming a princess."

She groaned. In the past few minutes of conversation she'd managed to forget her predicament. "Cleo already mentioned that I'm a college professor. I teach women's studies at a university in eastern Washington state."

"Tell me about your mom."

Zara's entire face changed. Rafe watched as the embarrassment fled, replaced by a look of love so private that he nearly looked away.

"She was amazing." Zara sounded wistful as she spoke. "So beautiful and talented. She was a dancer for years. After she had me, she taught dance and got involved with community theater. Eventually she started directing."

"Do you look like her?"

"No." She drew her knees to her chest, careful to keep her nightgown and robe covering every inch of her, then rested her chin on her knees. "I suppose I'm tall like her, and skinny. But she had curves, which I do not. And she was graceful. I can barely walk through a room without knocking things over."

"Tell me about growing up."

Her mouth pulled straight, then twisted. "We moved around a lot. I think my mom had a giant case of wanderlust. Part of it might have been to keep King Hassan from finding her, but most of it was that she liked to be in different places. I think in a perfect world, she would have been part of a dance troupe that traveled all the time."

"But she wasn't. And she had a child."

Zara nodded, her long, wavy hair swaying slightly with the movement. Earlier that day, she'd worn her hair back in a braid, but tonight it was loose. Rafe found himself wanting to slip his fingers through the strands to find out if it was as soft as it looked. He wanted to breathe in the scent of her hair, of her body, and taste every part of her with—

He grabbed hold of his wayward desire and firmly

quashed it. Zara was his responsibility. No way was he going to give in to an urge, no matter how strong.

"She really tried to stay in one place," Zara told him. "But it wasn't her nature. She used to apologize when she needed to move on. I was constantly the new kid, which was really hard for me. I didn't make friends easily. So I escaped into books. Growing up I learned to lose myself in a good story. I spent a lot of time in the library."

Her world sounded lonely. He could relate to that. "What about dance classes? Didn't you say your mother was a teacher?"

She laughed. "She was a fabulous instructor, but I wasn't kidding about being a klutz. For a while my mom took it as a personal insult that her own flesh and blood couldn't perform a few basic dance steps. Eventually she decided to give up and stop torturing us both."

"I doubt it was that bad."

Zara sat up enough to make an X on her chest. "I'm not lying. It was horrible. Cleo did better than me at dance class, but she was never that interested."

"How did Cleo come to be with you?" he asked.

Zara shrugged. "Cleo always makes a joke about it, talking like she was a puppy picked up at the pound. Unfortunately, it's not all that far from the truth. I don't remember the details—I was only fourteen and not really paying attention. There was some kind of temporary crisis in the foster care system with too many kids and not enough homes. An appeal was made to the public. My mom thought it would be fun for me to have a younger sister. One day Cleo was there.''

She smiled slightly, as if at a memory. ''We didn't really get along at first. She was ten and angry at the world. She never knew her father, and her mother did drugs and couldn't keep a job. Cleo grew up in shelters and on the street. She used to hoard food and refuse to talk. At night she would cry in her sleep. The next time Fiona moved us, Cleo came along and that was it. There was no formal adoption. Eventually Cleo and I became close. We might not have a lot in common, but we were each other's best friend.''

''The state never came looking for her?''

''Not really. I'm still not sure what happened—if her paperwork got lost or if they couldn't find us. By the time Cleo was fourteen we were in Arizona, then California after that. Fiona died when I was twenty. Cleo was sixteen. We stayed together, doing our best not to draw attention to ourselves. We were afraid Social Services would take her away until she turned eighteen. Fortunately no one found out.''

''You raised her by yourself?''

Zara laughed. ''Cleo would get really annoyed if she heard you describe it that way. She was pretty grown-up. Way more street smart than I've ever been. She lived with me, and we looked out for each other.''

''You must have been in college by then.''

''I was. Fiona had insurance, which surprised us. She wasn't usually that much into the details. It was enough to pay for the rest of my education and Cleo's, if she'd wanted to go to school. But she wasn't that interested. Instead she went out and got a job.''

Hers was a normal world he couldn't relate to. Rafe supposed at one time he'd lived in a suburb with parents and maybe a dog, but he couldn't remember anything like that. All he could recall was being alone.

"What made you decide to go into teaching?" he asked.

"I didn't know what I wanted to do," she admitted. "When I applied to graduate school, I got into a program where the grad students teach a freshman class. It was my first experience in front of a group. Initially I was nervous, but then I found I really liked it."

He wondered how many of her students had a crush on her.

She raised her head and stared out into the darkness of the sea. "I live in farm country," she said quietly. "Lots of rolling hills of wheat and canola. There isn't all that much to do and the closest big city is nearly a hundred miles away. I can't imagine a place more different than Bahania."

"Or the palace," he reminded her.

"I don't want to think about it. This isn't anything I'm prepared for. I have no social skills or diplomatic training. What if I offend some important person and create an international incident?"

"They're harder to create than you might think. The greater danger is that some sheik is going to take a liking to you and kidnap you."

She laughed. "Oh, yeah, that's *so* likely. Besides as my temporary bodyguard, you're supposed to prevent that sort of thing."

"I'll do my best."

Which was the truth. Equally true was his desire to kidnap her himself. A couple of weeks in a private paradise would go a long way toward easing his throbbing need. Rafe studied Zara's delicate profile and wondered why this particular woman got to him. What arrangement of scents, sights and sounds made him want to forget his permanent rule of never getting involved with anyone who wasn't a player? Reminding himself that she claimed to be innocent—and why would a woman lie about that?—not to mention the daughter of a king, ought to be enough to keep him in line.

"Speaking of sheiks…" She turned and looked at him. "Why were you dressed in traditional desert clothes earlier today?"

He didn't want to answer that question, so he distracted her with one of his own. "Why are you a virgin?"

Chapter Six

Zara's feet hit the balcony floor with a thud. "I can't believe you're asking me that," she said, horrified, humiliated and barely able to speak. Heat flared on her face. Once again she was grateful for the darkness. "It's a very personal matter and not one I'm willing to discuss with you." Or anyone.

Rafe didn't look the least bit intimidated by her outburst or chagrined by her response. "You're the one who brought it up," he reminded her. "It's not the sort of information a guy forgets."

"Well, you should forget it. It's none of your business."

Unless he wanted to make it his business.

A zing of anticipation zipped through her midsection. What if Rafe found her...attractive? Zara dismissed the thought as soon as it appeared. Daydreams were fine when one was alone and the object of one's musings was a famous movie star. But this was real life. She had no business fantasizing about someone who actually existed. Especially not someone like him.

"Come on, Zara. You can tell me. How did an attractive, sexy woman like you avoid the come-ons of all those professor types?"

Sexy? He thought she was sexy? Before the zing could turn into something bigger and better, she reminded herself that he was being nice to her because it was his job. If Rafe was interested in one of the Paxton sisters he would be far more likely to go seek out Cleo. Men had been sniffing around her since Cleo had turned fourteen. While her sister had been on every guy's wish list, Zara had spent her weekends alone.

"There have been fewer come-ons than one might think."

"I don't believe you."

She glared at him. "Are you deliberately trying to humiliate me?"

"No. I'm deliberately trying to understand."

She stood and walked to the balcony, standing with her back to the sea. She didn't think he was being mean. A part of her wanted to believe that Rafe found her attractive. She sighed. Was this before or after aliens landed and delivered the secret to the universe?

"I never had much luck with dating," she said, staring at a spot over his head. "I was too tall, too smart and too skinny. Plus with all the moving around, I never exactly found a place where I fit in.

I didn't date in high school, and in college I was slow to make friends. About the time I finally had a group of people I trusted and a few boys who might have been interested, my mom died. Not only did I have to deal with that, but Cleo moved in with me. We had the combination of our loss and our fear of being discovered and her taken away. That pretty much nipped any potential relationships in the bud."

She crossed her arms over her chest. "Are you sure you want to hear this?"

"Absolutely."

She wanted to ask why. No doubt he was simply being polite. No doubt she should excuse herself and head back to her room. Except she enjoyed standing in the dark, talking with him. As Cleo was forever reminding her—she was way too much of a dreamer.

"I moved to Washington State to attend graduate school," she said. "So it was a while before I met people and got settled. There were a few guys, but no one special. Then I met Jon."

Rafe stretched his legs out in front of him. "Why don't I like this guy?"

"I don't know. He was very nice. Charming. Funny. He was an administrator at the college. We got along really well." She hesitated. No way was she going to tell Rafe that there hadn't been any passion between them. At least not on his side. "He changed me," she said instead. "I can't explain it. He made suggestions about my clothes—things that helped me feel more attractive."

Rafe stared at her. "A guy had suggestions about

your clothes? I assume this was more than asking you to take them off.''

''Of course. He never—'' She pressed her lips together. ''We didn't exactly, you know.''

''You weren't lovers.''

She closed her eyes, then forced herself to open them and meet his steady gaze. ''No. We were not.'' She cleared her throat. ''But there were other compensations and when Jon proposed, I accepted.''

Rafe sprang to his feet. ''You married the guy?''

''Not exactly.''

He stalked over to the railing and stood next to her. Really, the man was unreasonably tall. She hated that she had to tilt her head to look at him.

''We were engaged for a time.''

''How long?''

''Two years.''

''Two years!'' His voice exploded into the quiet of the night. ''Are you kidding?'' He spoke more quietly. ''You were engaged to this guy for two years and you never slept with him.''

''We wanted to wait.''

''For what? Nuclear winter?''

''Some people prefer the sanctity of marriage.''

Rafe shook his head. ''This afternoon you were complaining that if you were really a princess you would never get the chance to have sex. That doesn't sound like a 'sanctity of marriage' argument to me.''

She sighed. ''All right. Perhaps I didn't agree with what we were doing, but I could hardly force the man. By that time I was twenty-six, nearly twenty-seven and I was very ready to see what all the fuss was about.''

''Did you confront this bozo?''

''No. Three weeks before the wedding, Jon told me that he wanted to break off our engagement. He'd been wrestling with some issues that could no longer be ignored.''

Rafe swore. ''He was gay, right?''

Zara's mouth dropped open. ''How did you know?''

''The guy helped you pick out clothes. Most men can barely dress themselves and if it's more complicated than a navy-blue suit or jeans, forget it. Plus, going two years without sex, especially when he had a hot fiancée who was more than willing—it doesn't make sense any other way.''

Hot? Zara wanted to ask him if he'd really said the word. Did Rafe think she was hot? Her? She'd never really developed breasts, not serious ones like Cleo's. She was tall and skinny, not short, curvy and irresistible. She must not have heard him correctly.

''So what happened when he told you?'' he asked.

It took her a second to figure out what he was talking about. ''I was crushed,'' she admitted. ''And humiliated. The university is in a small town. Everyone knew, and it didn't take them long to find out why. When I was ready to start dating again, I felt like every guy worried that I'd turn him gay.''

Rafe chuckled. ''Not likely.''

''I guess, but I'd also reached an age where being a virgin was strange. The situation is only getting worse with time. The last two men I went out with disappeared when I confessed all. What if I really am Hassan's daughter? I'll never get a date again and if I do, no one is going to sleep with me. Being a virgin princess is not my idea of a good time.''

Rafe laughed. He threw back his head and enjoyed the moment, ignoring her sniff of indignation.

''Easy for you to have a good chuckle,'' she grumbled. ''You aren't the one who could live her life in a fishbowl. You aren't the one who has to explain this after a few dates.''

''You know, you could just wait for marriage,'' Rafe offered helpfully.

''I don't think I'm ever going to get married,'' she said. ''Not if I don't date, which is getting more and more difficult. It's only going to be worse, now. Besides, I thought it might be nice to have a little experience. I'm not interested in sleeping with an entire football team, but I *would* like to see at least one guy naked before I die.''

Rafe couldn't believe they were having this conversation. For one thing, he didn't think there were any more twenty-eight-year-old virgins left. Which proved Zara's point—not that he was about to tell her that. For another, he was damned tempted to volunteer his services. She was welcome to see him naked anytime she wanted. She could even touch. Of course then he would want to touch back, and that was only going to lead to trouble.

''You have the strangest look on your face,'' she told him.

''I'll bet.''

Just thinking about her looking at him was making

him hard. This whole situation was going to be nothing but trouble. He could feel it down to his bones.

"You're going to have to be careful," he said. "Once word gets out that you're Hassan's daughter, everything is going to change."

She turned and faced the water. "We don't know that I *am* his daughter."

"Do you really have doubts?"

She slowly shook her head. "I want to, but I know it in my heart."

"I agree with you on that one. Which means the media is going to be all over you. You'll become the flavor of the month, and that's going to bring out all kinds of men. They'll want to take advantage of you."

He winced as he spoke the old-fashioned phrase, but didn't know another way to say what he meant.

Zara smiled. "I have nothing to offer. Being Hassan's daughter isn't going to change that."

"You're wrong. You'll have connections to the royal family. Your father is a king, you'll be a princess. I'm sure Hassan will make you rich in your own right."

She rested her forearms on the balcony and leaned forward. "It sounded better from half a world away. Back home I could dream about the possibilities. Now it's all just scary." She turned her head and glanced at him. "I don't suppose I could persuade him not to give me any money."

"I don't think so. The king is pretty stubborn."

"Great. So I get to be popular for all the wrong reasons. How am I supposed to know if the people I meet like me for me or because I'm Hassan's daughter?''

"I can't answer that." He would be far better at planning a kidnapping or taking out a foreign government.

Zara nodded. "It's really late, and we should both try to sleep. You've been really sweet to stay out here and talk to me, but I'm sure you'd rather be in bed."

She'd read his mind, he thought. Unfortunately they were thinking about two different kinds of "in bed." She meant alone and he wanted to be with her.

"Good night, Zara."

"Night."

He waited until she walked back into her bedroom before sitting back on the bench. As he stared at the stars in the desert sky, he willed his body to return to normal.

But the need was slow to leave him and it was nearly dawn before he finally closed his eyes and slept.

The Princess Sabra...aka Sabrina...did *not* make good on her promise to lend her new sister clothes. Instead, the following afternoon shortly before two there was a knock on the suite door.

Zara stopped pacing long enough to watch Cleo answer it. So far she'd had a short but intense meeting with her father, and someone from his office had delivered a thick pile of reports, books and brochures on Bahania and the ruling family. Zara couldn't shake the feeling that she was going to get grilled on the information sometime later.

"Maybe it's the guy who's gonna give you your pop quiz," Cleo said cheerfully as she opened the door.

But the people who waited in the hallway obviously had nothing to do with tests or questions. Three loudly speaking, broadly gesturing French women entered the suite followed by servants pushing large clothing racks. Someone brought in a pallet of shoe boxes. There were also dozens of shopping bags filled with lingerie and knits and hat boxes.

"I am Marie," a petite redhead said as she approached Zara and smiled. "Ah, you are the one. I see the likeness." She winked broadly. "Nothing is to be said yet, I know. You can trust Marie. And this beauty is your sister."

After squeezing Zara's hand, Marie glided over to Cleo and embraced her. She fingered Cleo's short, spiky hair.

"The color is amazing. Natural I am thinking, yes?"

Cleo nodded. Her blue eyes widened as she took in all the clothes. Marie followed her gaze.

"Ah. You have noticed my humble offerings. Princess Sabra called this morning and explained that you two had need of everything. And there is the dinner tonight. You must look perfect."

Zara had been doing her best not to think about the state dinner. King Hassan had promised that there would be a protocol meeting later that afternoon. Zara preferred to skip the entire event, but the king wouldn't hear of it.

She looked at the racks of clothes. There were formal gowns, plus more casual clothing. "I don't understand. I'll admit that Cleo and I each need a dress, but you've brought a lot more than that."

Marie beamed. "The princess insisted that you completely redo your wardrobes. She said you were from a much colder climate and were not prepared for the heat of Bahania."

Zara pressed her lips together. At least Sabrina had been tactful. What she could have said instead was that the woman who might be her new half sister dressed in bargain-basement chic. Zara didn't think she'd ever spent more than a hundred dollars on an outfit, with the possible exception of one of her suits. Cleo preferred in-style and cheap to classics that would last more than a season.

Zara moved to the rack and fingered a pink chiffon dress. Her movements caused the price tag to flutter slightly. She gasped and hastily released the fabric. The dress cost twelve thousand dollars. *Twelve thousand dollars.* That would practically pay for a new car.

"We can't," Zara said, tucking her hands behind her back. "This isn't right."

Cleo frowned. "Zara, what's the problem?"

Zara nodded at the rack. Cleo looked at a couple of dresses, sighing audibly when she brushed against a midnight blue velvet gown. Her breath caught a second later. She looked at her sister.

"I prefer to spend my take-home pay on rent and food, but everyone has different priorities," Cleo said brightly, but Zara could see the shock in her eyes.

"My thoughts exactly."

Marie looked confused. She exchanged an unintelligible conversation with her two assistants. Zara had taken French in high school, but her only memories of the language included telling someone her name and asking the time. Not that she would be able to understand the answer to the question.

Marie motioned to the clothes. "You are not happy with the quality of our things? I assure you, these are the finest designer originals. The styles are both contemporary and flattering. If you would be so kind as to tell me what I can change, I will do so." She appeared more worried than annoyed.

"It's not your clothes," Zara said. "We can't afford these ourselves, and I'm not comfortable accepting them as a gift."

This statement produced more rapid-fire French, which ended when Marie clapped her hands together. "Ms. Paxton, Princess Sabra was very explicit. You and your sister were to have all new clothes. The bill was to go on the palace account. If you refuse, she will think you were not satisfied. She might decide to dismiss me. Without the patronage of the royal family, my boutique would not survive." She shrugged. "So you see, you must accept her gift. For my sake."

Cleo inched close. "It's a darned good argument."

"One I'm not sure I believe," Zara whispered back.

"We have to have dresses for tonight. What if we just take those and tell her we're too tired to shop for anything else?"

Zara nodded. Cleo's plan made sense. She supposed that as the king's daughter she would be expected to dress a certain way. Obviously her outlet mall days were behind her. But she couldn't make too many changes at once without going crazy.

"Let's start with dresses for tonight," Zara told Marie. "That may take a while. We'll deal with the rest of it later."

Marie sighed with obvious relief. "Yes, of course."

She clapped her hands. Several bags and one of the racks disappeared. Her assistants began sorting through the shoe boxes.

"Princess Sabra guessed on sizes. She trusted my judgment in what would be appropriate. We've brought shoes and evening bags, as well."

Marie began flipping through dresses. She tossed several toward one assistant and other dresses toward another. Then she ordered Cleo and Zara into their bedrooms to try things on.

Zara found out right away that Marie and her assistant didn't believe in modesty. Zara found herself standing by her bed and wearing only her panties. She tried to casually cross her arms over her small chest, but neither woman noticed. Instead they were discussing the various attributes of the dresses.

"You are very thin," Marie said. "You can get away with something more dramatic." She reached up and pulled Zara's arms to her sides and frowned at her chest. "Your breasts are small, but we can help that with a bit of padding, yes?"

Mortified beyond words, Zara could only gulp air. Marie didn't seem to notice. Instead she fingered Zara's long hair and smiled. "We will put this up, I think. You don't wear much makeup. With your skin it is not necessary. But tonight, a little extra will make you shine. Now for the dresses.''

They whipped them on and off her with lightning speed. Beaded gowns, velvet dresses, garments made from silk so delicate it was more like gossamer wings. At last Marie found one she liked and allowed Zara to look into the mirror. She nearly fell over.

The dress was a halter style, beaded and gold. The color shimmered with each movement, catching and reflecting light. But what stunned Zara was the front, which was cut down nearly to her waist. Straps of heavy fabric covered her breasts, but if she turned too quickly, she popped out, like bread from a toaster.

Marie clucked. ''We would have to take this in a little and use the tape.''

Zara felt practically naked. ''Tape?''

''It goes on the side of the halter, to keep the fabric pressed against your skin.''

''Ah, how do you get it off?''

Marie stared at her as if she were incredibly stupid. ''You rip it quickly. It barely hurts.''

Zara tried to smile, although she was feeling a little nauseous. She had a bad feeling that what might barely hurt Marie would render her unconscious.

''Maybe a different style would be better,'' she murmured.

They went through a half dozen more dresses until they found a simple slip dress in iridescent bronze silk. The material skimmed over her body, giving the illusion of curves, except on top. The color made her skin glow and she felt almost dressed.

"I like this one," she said, wishing there was a way to add about two inches to her chest.

Marie nodded her agreement. "Yes. It's very pretty. There are some bronze sandals." She snapped out an order and sent the assistant scurrying.

Zara looked at herself from all angles. "This is great. Maybe I should ask Sabrina if this dress is all right," she murmured, hoping her new almost-sister wouldn't scratch her eyes out instead of giving an opinion.

"She will love it. While you do that, I'll check on your sister."

"Great."

The dress was exactly the right length, Zara noted as she followed Marie back into the living room. The assistant handed her a pair of strappy, high-heeled sandals that fitted perfectly. Zara stepped out into the hallway, then paused when she realized she didn't have a clue as to where she was supposed to go. How did people in the palace keep track of each other? Was there a palace operator or maybe a beeper system?

Before she could figure out what to do, a door opened a few feet down the hall. She almost wasn't surprised when Rafe stepped out.

"What is it with you?" she asked before he could speak. "Do you have a light that goes off in your room if I leave mine?"

He looked her up and down. "You look nice. Is that for tonight?"

His compliment made her feel all soft and gooey inside. Then she remembered the very intimate conversation they'd had the previous night and she wasn't sure if she was supposed to be embarrassed or not. Rafe felt like the only normal person in the tornado that was her current life.

"A woman showed up with a bunch of clothes for Cleo and me. We're picking out dresses for the dinner." She held out the skirt of the gown. "I thought maybe I'd ask Sabrina if this dress was all right. There are a couple of others that would work, but I like this one best. Still, I'm not sure I'm going in the right direction. I don't have a lot of experience with formal state dinners."

"She's out with her husband and won't be back for a couple of hours. I'd be happy to give you my opinion."

Zara eyed him doubtfully. "Do you know anything about these kind of functions?"

"I've been to dozens. Show me what else you're considering."

This had been a stupid idea, Rafe told himself fifteen minutes later as he stood in the center of Zara's bedroom and watched her model a strapless number in emerald green. Even though she disappeared into the bathroom to change, he could *hear* clothing rustle as she dressed, which was practically the same as *seeing* her change into each gown. The cut of the current one made it impossible for her to be wearing anything but panties underneath. Which made him think about joining her in the bathroom the next time she disappeared. Which made him think about very personal contact. Which made him hard.

He swore silently and shifted, then sank into a corner chair. With luck, the combination of shadows and her relative innocence would keep her from figuring out that he was aroused.

Zara turned back and forth in front of the full-length mirror. She put her hands on her waist and sighed.

"I don't know if this looks weird," she muttered. "Is my neck too long? Do I look like a skinny bird?"

"You look beautiful."

She met his gaze in the mirror. "Why do I suddenly think that being nice to me is part of the job?"

"It's not in the contract. Zara, you look great in that dress. So far I've liked all of them. What's the problem?"

"I don't know. I want to look—" She shook her head. "I guess I want to look like someone else."

"Why?"

"Because. I'm just ordinary. My skin is a decent color and it's clear, so that's nice. I guess I like my eyes, but my mouth is weird."

He thought it was full and sensual. Her mouth made him think of kissing…intimate kissing. It made him wonder how her lips would feel on his body, his hands tangling in her hair as she—

Down boy, he told himself.

The bedroom door opened and Cleo breezed in. "I've found it," she announced, grinning.

Zara looked at her sister and visibly wilted. Cleo's dress was similar to Zara's but in a deep cobalt blue that matched her eyes. The bustier bodice hugged lush curves that threatened to spill out with every breath.

The straight skirt skimmed over Cleo's full hips before falling to the floor. Zara looked cool and elegant, like an ice princess. Cleo was a walking, breathing invitation to have sex.

The two sisters looked at each other. Cleo's smile faded. "Oh, no. We can't be twins. If that's the dress you want to wear, I'll find something else."

"Are you kidding?" Zara tugged at her loose bodice. "Even with padding, I'll never do this dress justice. There's another one I like just as well. I'll wear that."

"Are you sure?"

Zara managed a smile. "Cleo, you have to wear that. You look so fabulous that no one will notice me, which is exactly how I want things."

"Okay. Great."

Cleo saw him and gave a little wave. "You're taking this protecting thing a little too seriously, aren't you, Rafe?"

"Just here to give my opinion."

"Sure."

Her expression turned knowing, making him wonder if she'd figured out that Zara got to him.

Cleo sashayed out the door, closing it behind her. Zara covered her face in her hands.

"Did you see her?" she asked. "I can't believe it. She has the most incredible body and I'm left with all the appeal of a green bean."

"That's not true."

She lowered her hands. "You're being nice and I appreciate it, but we both know the truth. All the padding in the world isn't going to disguise my short-comings.''

Without thinking, he rose to his feet and crossed the room to stand in front of her. ''There's nothing wrong with you.'' He turned her so that they were both facing the mirror. ''What would you change?''

''Everything.''

''I wouldn't.''

Without considering the intelligence of the move—or the potential consequences—he spun her toward him, pulled her close and kissed her.

Chapter Seven

Rafe couldn't possibly be kissing her, Zara told herself, trying to stay calm. But even as the thought formed, his arms came around her body and pulled her close while his mouth settled on hers. It really felt like a kiss.

His lips were firm and warm, yet so tender she wanted to melt. His height allowed her to feel delicate and feminine as she snuggled in his embrace. She placed her hands on his shoulders, savoring the tense muscles shifting against her fingertips. Then he moved his mouth, and she couldn't think anymore. Not when sweet sparks exploded in her chest, making her want with an intensity she'd never felt before.

His tongue swept against her bottom lip. Instinctively she parted for him, then waited expectantly for the first, intimate touch. He didn't disappoint her. After tracing the inside of her lower lip, making her shiver, he moved closer and swept inside.

The first brush of his tongue nearly made her faint. Hot pleasure filled her body, starting in her chest, then moving lower. Her skin seemed to tighten and become more sensitized. She was aware of his hands on her body—one at the small of her back, one higher, on bare skin.

His fingers moved in time with his tongue, back and forth, around and around. Initially she'd touched him because they were kissing and she could, but now she clung to him. That whole bone-dissolve thing had started up again, and she knew she was in danger of falling.

Then there was the matter of her breasts. As small as they might be, they were exquisitely sensitive. As the passion grew, Zara felt her nipples tighten. When Rafe shifted, grinding his chest against her modest curves, she gasped from the contact. The combination of pleasure and tension was more than she was used to. She desperately wanted him to jerk down the zipper in the back of her dress and cover her breasts with his hands. At that moment she didn't even care that they were small and unimpressive—she simply wanted him to touch them…to touch her…all of her.

Instead of reading her mind, he cupped her face, as if he needed to keep her from running while they kissed. The swirl of tongues, the press of bodies, was nearly more than she could stand. The room tilted slightly, but Zara found she didn't care about things like staying conscious. What did that matter when compared with the glory of Rafe's kiss?

She slipped her hands down to his side, then slid around to his back. He was so strong, so muscled. She wanted to see him without clothes; she wanted to touch him everywhere. She wanted—

He broke the kiss and nipped on her bottom lip. Before she could do more than gasp, he moved lower, kissing, nibbling, and licking his way over her jaw and down her throat. She held her breath, desperately hoping that he might have read her mind. Lower and lower until he reached the loose fabric over her breasts.

Instead of reaching for the zipper, he simply shoved the bodice down, baring her to the waist. Before she could protest, or cover herself, he took one nipple in his mouth and sucked.

She felt the fire all the way down to her toes. Rational thought fled, as did her ability to breathe. She could only gasp as he teased the sensitive bud and drove her wild with passion. Her thighs trembled and ached. Between them a throbbing began, one that made her remember that her very large bed was only a few feet away.

Rafe pulled away and swore. She thought he was going to step back, but instead he pulled her dress back up over her breasts, then jerked her against him and kissed her frantically. His fingers dug into her scalp, his tongue thrust against hers and his body melded with her own. She felt the hardness of his muscles, then a different kind of hardness. One that made her think he was as turned on as she was.

He groaned in his throat and drew back. Zara blinked several times. There was definitely fire in his blue eyes. Fire and wanting. Could this incredible passion be about her?

He stalked to the glass doors leading to the balcony and stared out at the horizon. "That shouldn't have happened," he said quietly.

"But it did." She cleared her throat. She couldn't stop thinking about that *ridge* she'd felt. "Rafe, are you, um, armed?"

He turned to face her. "What?"

"Do you have a gun?" She motioned vaguely toward his trousers without actually looking there.

One corner of his mouth quirked up in a shadow of a smile. "No."

"So you're um..." Her voice trailed off. "You were, um, *interested* in what we were doing?"

His gaze narrowed. "What are you trying to find out?"

She couldn't actually say the words. Heat flared on her cheeks. "You know. I sort of felt...something."

He shook his head. "I can't believe you're asking that. Yes, I was aroused. I wanted you. I still want you."

Happiness filled her. She felt light enough to float. She hadn't been wrong. He'd really been hard—and for her.

He walked toward her and stopped a couple of feet in front of her. After putting his hands on her shoulders, he shook her slightly.

"Don't look so surprised," he told her. "There's nothing wrong with your body. In fact, I think everything about it's just right. Of course I want to make love with you."

It was the best thing any man had ever said to her. She nearly swooned. Even as air refused to fill her lungs, she had a very clear image of the two of them in bed. They would be naked, moving together. She got a little vague at that point, but Rafe was the kind of man who knew things. He would make her first time wonderful. In fact—

"Whatever you're thinking, you can just forget it," he said bluntly.

"Huh?"

He dropped his arms to his sides. "I mean it, Zara. There's not going to be one damn thing between us. I should never have kissed you."

"I can't quite bring myself to agree with you," she murmured before she could stop herself.

He continued as if she hadn't spoken. "You're a princess. I'm your temporary bodyguard. My job is to keep you safe from every kind of threat. That means the sexual ones—even if they come from me."

She planted her hands on her hips. "Why? We obviously both enjoyed kissing. What's so horrible about that?"

He dismissed her with a quick jerk of his fingers. "We both know where we were going."

Her elation grew. Really? They'd been heading to bed? He'd thought they'd been about to do it? The frustration of finally being with a man who really wanted her and yet refused to give in to temptation made her temper flare.

"I don't understand," she told him. "In all the movies I've seen, the bodyguard always sleeps with the client."

"This isn't a movie," he growled. "There are a lot of reasons why I'm not giving in to temptation."

He continued talking but she wasn't listening. Temptation? Rafe—the walking, breathing hunk who could have any woman he wanted on this planet and probably several others—thought she was a temptation? Wow.

"Zara, you're not paying attention."

She smiled. "I know." He sounded so serious when she just wanted to freeze-frame the moment so she could have it always.

He crooked his finger and pushed his knuckle against her chin. "I'm trying to make a point here. What would have happened if we'd continued?"

She was a little fuzzy on that part of things, which was her point.

"Things would have gotten hot and heavy pretty fast," he said when she didn't speak. "About two seconds after that, your dress lady would have come strolling back into the bedroom. Want to think about that for a second?"

Zara most definitely did not. She'd forgotten about the fitting. "Oh."

"Yeah. Oh. Scandal isn't pretty. Trust me on this. And while I finally have your attention, listen to this. I'm not some handsome prince looking for true love. I don't believe in commitments or forever. I don't believe in settling down. I live for the moment and then move on. I'm about the worst kind of man for you, so stay clear of me."

Her embarrassment returned. She pulled free of his light touch and turned away. "No one said anything about commitments," she mumbled. "I thought we were talking about sex."

"I doubt you can separate them."

She spun toward him. "I wouldn't know that, would I? Just once I would like to meet a single man who would be willing to make love with me. That's all I want. Just one guy. Everyone else on the planet seems to be having a fine time in bed and I can't even come close to getting naked."

She walked to the far side of the room. The vanity drawer just below the mirror was partially open. She slammed it for good measure. While she couldn't regret the kissing, Rafe's reaction was taking all the fun out of it. She *wasn't* interested in a commitment. Okay, maybe she would be one day. After all she'd always wanted a husband and family. But not yet. Not before she'd actually done the wild thing.

"There's another, more compelling reason I chose not to give in to lust," he said casually, as if they were talking about the weather. "I intend to keep my head right where it belongs."

Zara glanced at him. "What are you talking about?"

"You're the daughter of a ruling monarch. Men like the king have a thing against their virgin daughters being defiled. Especially not by the hired help. Punishment is swift and permanent."

Her eyes widened. "That's crazy. He wouldn't cut off your head."

Rafe shrugged. "If you don't believe me, ask him yourself."

With that he turned and headed for her bedroom door.

"They'd cut off his head?" Cleo asked later that afternoon when Zara recounted her conversation with Rafe. "That is so cool!"

Zara hadn't gone into all the details. In fact she'd left out the most interesting bits. The part about Rafe kissing her and having physical proof of his arousal. She still wasn't ready to tell that to anyone...not even her sister.

"I don't think I share your opinion of the information," Zara said glumly. "I already have trouble getting dates. What's going to happen when the men I meet find out that the price of having sex with me is death? They're hardly going to be jumping for joy."

They were in Cleo's room, sitting on her bed. A light snack had been delivered by a servant just a few minutes ago, along with a written note from Sabrina, telling them what time to be ready and that they would be escorted to the event. Zara didn't like the fact that Sabrina had written rather than called. It didn't bode well for her future relationship with her new half sister. Like she didn't already have enough problems.

"You don't have to tell every guy you meet the truth," Cleo said, then picked up a slice of melon and took a bite.

"If they meet me here, they're already going to know I'm the king's daughter."

Zara fingered a cracker, but found she couldn't actually eat. Nerves were doing tai chi in her stomach. Between her passionate encounter with Rafe, her trepidation about meeting the rest of her potential family, the formal dinner and Sabrina's cold shoulder, she found herself wanting to head back to the States and pretend that this had never happened.

"Maybe your run of back luck in the man department is about to change," Cleo said cheerfully. "It couldn't get worse."

"Don't tempt fate by saying that." Zara nibbled on the cracker. "I can't believe how complicated this all is. Rafe also told me that men were going to be interested in me because of my position as Hassan's daughter."

"Well, duh." Cleo shook her head. "You are so unprepared to handle this."

Zara knew that her sister meant the comment kindly, but it still stung. Sometimes she really hated that Cleo was so "man" experienced. No doubt tonight she would create a sensation. What would it be like to be so incredibly attractive to men? Just once Zara would like to think that someone could find her irresistible, too.

"I'll have to be careful," Zara said. "It's going to be strange not knowing if a man is interested in me for myself or for my connections." She grimaced. "Actually, I already have that answer. I'll know exactly what he's interested in."

Cleo scooted close and touched her arm. "Zara, you're too hard on yourself. Just because you've picked stupid men in the past doesn't mean there aren't dozens of wonderful guys who would think you're incredible. Because you are. Someday you're going to meet the right guy and he's going to knock your socks off and you're going to make him not care about getting his head chopped off.''

Zara laughed. "Oh, sure. Who would risk death to sleep with me? I couldn't get anyone to do it before."

"It'll happen. You'll see."

Zara appreciated Cleo's support, but didn't believe a word of it. As for someone knocking off her socks, Rafe had done a darn good job. She'd also aroused him. But apparently not enough. He'd practically left skid marks in his haste to warn her off.

Someone knocked at their door precisely on time. Zara smoothed down the front of the bronze-colored dress she'd slipped into and headed for the door. Marie and her staff had worked magic, nipping and tucking the fabric until the soft folds created the illusion of curves. A strapless padded bra gave her a couple of inches on top.

Nearly an hour and a half before, Renee had arrived with a suitcase full of cosmetics, followed by Eric who did hair. Between the two of them, Zara had been transformed. Her long hair had been piled high on her head in an elaborate style that swept up and around. A servant had brought a diamond tiara, along with several jewelry choices. Cleo had nearly drooled in delight. The sparkling diamonds and sapphires made Zara nervous and as she reached for the door handle, she rubbed her fingers against the diamond drop earrings she'd chosen.

Rafe stood in the hall. He'd changed into a tuxedo,

which fitted him perfectly. No doubt his association with a royal family required formal wear.

Her gaze lingered on his handsome face, most especially his mouth. She could instantly recall how his lips felt on hers and the way she'd trembled in his embrace.

Rafe smiled. "You look good."

"Thanks. You, too."

She winced as soon as the words passed her lips. Could that have sounded more stupid? But Rafe didn't say anything to make her feel bad. Instead he stepped into the living room and glanced at his watch.

"We have to be at the reception anteroom in ten minutes."

"If that's a comment about me being late, you can forget it," Cleo said breezily. "I'm hardly the kind of girl to be late for her first chance to meet real, live handsome princes."

Cleo glided into the room, her eyes bright with humor and anticipation. Zara had been caught up in wondering if anyone she knew had ever actually been in an "anteroom" when she registered her sister's appearance.

On the one hand, she'd meant what she'd said about Cleo's beauty keeping people distracted so they wouldn't notice anything else. On the other hand, she felt like the country mouse come to town.

Cleo's cobalt-blue dress clung to every luscious curve, no padding required. The shimmering fabric caught the light, reflecting and dazzling as Cleo's breasts strained to the point of threatening to spill out. It wasn't enough of a display to be in bad taste, but it was enough that men were going to be catching their breath in private expectation.

Eric had styled Cleo's short hair into soft curls that framed her round face. Sapphire and diamond earrings decorated her ear lobes, while a matching bracelet glittered around her wrist.

Zara waited uncomfortably for Rafe to fall under her sister's spell, but after a brief word of greeting, he turned away from Cleo and motioned for the door.

"If you ladies are ready?"

Could he really not be attracted to Cleo? Zara remembered his arousal and felt a thrill of excitement. Had she finally found a man who was interested in her for her? Then she reminded herself that Rafe wasn't interested in her at all. He'd made it completely clear that he didn't do relationships.

He held out an arm to each of them. Cleo instantly snuggled close, while Zara felt slightly awkward as he escorted them down the hall.

Her sister laughed. "Rafe, you're armed."

"I'm cautious."

Cleo looked around him. "Zara, the man takes his job seriously. You might want to remind your watchdog here that you wouldn't object to a man asking you to dance. Or is that a security breach?"

"Zara is free to do as she wishes," Rafe said calmly.

"Oh, I see. As long as she can do it with you watching." Cleo raised her eyebrows. "I wouldn't have taken you for that kind of guy. Somehow you strike me as someone who wants to be in the middle of the action, not standing on the sidelines observing.''

Zara knew that Cleo didn't mean anything by her conversation. She didn't know about the kiss so she couldn't see how embarrassing her comments were. Still Zara wished there was some way to change the subject. But before she could try anything, they turned a corner and entered the anteroom.

Over a dozen people stood in small groups, chatting with the ease of those who know each other well. The moment the three of them entered the arched doorway, the room went completely silent. Zara found herself the uncomfortable center of attention.

She glanced around, taking in several tall, dark and handsome men who most probably were the princes and her half brothers. Sabrina was there, standing next to another tall, good-looking man. Her husband? There were official looking types wearing tuxedos and medals or ribbons, along with elegantly clad women. In the center stood Hassan.

The king smiled broadly when he saw her. After handing his drink to one of his sons, he walked over, both hands extended.

''Zara. You are perfectly lovely this evening. I see you allowed me the pleasure of seeing you in a tiara. It was made for my great-grandmother's twenty-fifth birthday and has always been a favorite of mine.''

Still holding her hands, he leaned close and kissed her on her cheek. Then he turned his attention to Cleo and greeted her.

Zara noticed that everyone was still watching and that somehow Rafe had moved to the far side of the room where he spoke with Sabrina's husband. Sabrina didn't look very happy. Her gaze kept drifting to the tiara, and Zara wondered if her wearing it was significant in some way.

She found herself being introduced to the king's four sons. They were polite enough, but obviously far more interested in Cleo. In a matter of minutes two of them had pulled her sister away and were arguing over who had the pleasure of dining with her.

Hassan moved closer. "You look nervous, my daughter. Do not be concerned. This is a small event."

"I can't help being concerned that your definition of small is different from mine."

Hassan dismissed her concerns. "There are only a few hundred people here tonight."

Zara thought she might faint. "A few hundred?" That was way too many. "You're not going to say anything about me, are you? I mean about who I may be."

"Of course not. I want you to get used to being here first."

"I don't think that's going to happen." She looked longingly toward the door. "Maybe this should wait until after we've taken blood tests and have received the results. You know, just to be sure."

Hassan chuckled, then tucked her hand into the crook of his arm. "My delightful child, I *am* sure."

He led her around the anteroom and introduced her to everyone. Faces and names blurred. She thought that Sabrina's husband, Prince Kardal, seemed a little more friendly than his wife. The ambassador of El

Bahar had actually kissed her fingers. Talk about strange.

Just when she was able to breathe easily and tell herself that she might be able to survive the evening, a servant in formal dress appeared and announced that it was time for them to move into the main reception room.

Hassan led the way, heading for two ornately carved, arched doors. Unfortunately, her hand was still tucked in the crook of his arm, which meant she had to lead with him. Zara thought she might faint. She glanced around until she saw Rafe. He gave her a quick thumbs-up, before moving into line. She saw Cleo between two of the princes. Her sister looked blissfully happy.

Somewhere beyond the closed doors she heard music and conversation. Then the doors swung open as if by magic and they walked into a glittering ballroom.

There seemed to be a few thousand people rather than just a few hundred, but Zara supposed that was because she wasn't used to being the center of attention. So many faces, she thought as the entire crowd turned in their direction. Intellectually Zara knew it was because of Hassan and his family, not because of her, yet she couldn't help feeling as if she were being judged and found wanting. Then the people closest began to curtsy or bow, depending on their gender.

Curtsy? Zara swallowed. Should she have done that when she'd seen the king? What about with the princes and with Sabrina. Her stomach flopped around in uncomfortable spasms as worry made her clench her teeth. How many laws had she and Cleo already broken?

Someone spoke to Hassan, and the king turned away. Zara used the opportunity to slip free of him. Her thought was to duck back behind the royal family, but before she had taken more than a step, Rafe was at her side.

"You might want to pretend you're enjoying yourself," he murmured in her ear as he nodded at someone he knew.

She sighed. "Is it that obvious?"

"Let's just say that personal guests of the king don't usually walk into a room looking as if they're about to have a root canal."

"Actually, I'd rather have the dental work without Novocain than be here."

Rafe placed his hand on the small of her back. "Sorry but that's not an option. Prepare yourself to meet everyone who is anyone in Bahanian circles."

Her heart rate increased, and her palms began to sweat. "I can't. I never remember people's names."

"Try to find something distinctive about them as a memory aid. Things like Count Crook has a crooked nose."

"Is there a Count Crook?"

"No. I was making up an example."

She looked at him. "What happens if I break into hysterical laughter?"

"I'll be forced to throw water in your face."

She imagined herself wet and dripping. It wasn't

an attractive visual. "Okay. I'll try to keep the hysterics to a minimum."

"Think about the king. He's delighted to have you here. You wouldn't want to hurt his feelings."

She was far more concerned about the possibility of throwing up, but before she could share that with Rafe, Hassan had returned to her side. He ushered her into the crowd and began introducing her to people.

Zara got lost after the first three names. She tried Rafe's technique, but none of these perfectly groomed folks had distinguishing features. Every woman was more beautiful than the last, each man more refined and gentlemanly. Hassan was careful to say she was the daughter of a friend, but his tone of voice implied there was some secret between them. Zara hoped that no one thought she was his new mistress.

Zara nodded throughout the introductions. Rafe was always close, but not close enough to talk to. She smiled at men in traditional sheik garments, women in designer gowns, dignitaries in Savile Row suits, all the while hoping no one could tell she was from some podunk town in the Pacific Northwest and that before tonight she'd never worn a dress that cost more than a hundred dollars.

"Zara, I'd like you to meet the duke of Netherton," the king said as they paused in front of a fair-haired man in his mid-thirties.

"Your Highness, always a pleasure. Ms. Paxton, an honor."

Like several men before him, the duke brought her hand to his mouth and lightly kissed her fingers.

He was tall and blond with blue eyes. The description also fit Rafe, but he and the duke had little else in common. Where Rafe was broad and obviously muscled, the duke had a more slender build. Rafe's blue eyes were dark and forbidding, although tempting. The duke's eyes were light, his expression faintly cynical.

Zara wanted to duck and run. Instead she forced herself to smile. "I've never met a duke before. What is the correct way to address you?"

"Call me Byron." He winced slightly. "No poetry jokes, please. My mother was a fan of Lord Byron's work."

Zara's hackles rose slightly. The duke had been so smooth, she almost hadn't noticed the fact that he assumed she wouldn't recognize the name and be able to place it. She told herself not to take the fact personally. No doubt many people didn't know who Lord Byron was or how his romantic poetry had made an entire generation of women swoon.

Another man joined them. Hassan made introductions. Jean-Paul of a French last name she hadn't quite caught, murmured to her in a seductive tone of voice. He was darkly handsome. While he didn't have a title, he wasted no time in mentioning the family chateau that had been around for nearly five hundred years, along with vineyards and many wonderful paintings that she "simply had to come see."

Right, Zara thought, trying to see the humor in the situation. Next time she was touring through France she would stop by.

"May I bring you some champagne?" Jean-Paul asked.

Byron lightly clasped her hand in his. "Actually, she had already agreed to accompany me to the bar."

Hassan grinned broadly. "I will leave you two to fight over the lovely Zara." He patted her cheek, then strolled away.

Zara glanced around for Rafe and was pleased to see him hovering in the background. She sent him a silent plea for rescue, but he either didn't get it or didn't feel up to interfering. Instead he followed as both Jean-Paul and the duke led her to one of the bars set up in a corner of the room.

"Sparkling water," she said when it was their turn. Both men looked disapproving.

"Not champagne?" Jean-Paul asked.

"Not tonight." She needed to keep a clear head to navigate the potential disasters, not to mention that she already had the beginnings of a headache.

"I understand you recently met the king," Jean-Paul said when they'd all been served and had stepped away from the bar.

"Yes. My sister and I have only been in Bahania for a short time."

"You'd never met him before?" Byron asked. "There hadn't been any contact between you at all?"

"No."

Jean-Paul nodded encouragingly. "You are so lovely, Zara. Tell me what you do when you are not here charming us all with your smile?"

She nearly gagged. Did he expect her to buy in to that line? "I'm a professor of women's studies at a university in the Pacific Northwest."

Byron took a step closer, attempting to edge out

the Frenchman. "Is there anyone special in your life?"

Jean-Paul took a step closer. "There is now."

Zara moved back a bit.

Byron ignored him and focused on her. "I have enjoyed my many visits to your delightful country. I spent nearly a year there after I graduated from Oxford."

Jean-Paul stroked her face. "The only thing nearly as appealing as a woman such as yourself is the sight of the vineyards in the summer, after a light rain. The grapes sparkle in the sun. I cannot describe the smells—rich earth, the vines, their fruit. Like Bahania, France is a feast for the senses, eh? Not like a cold, dreary island."

Byron took her arm and drew her away. "Have you been to England? Our manor home is open to the public every Wednesday and alternate Saturdays. You might have seen it. The London residence is private, of course. If you—"

Jean-Paul took her other arm and tugged. "Have you seen the view from the garden. It's delightful and reminds me a little of France."

Byron tugged harder. "She doesn't want to go with you."

Jean-Paul frowned. "She doesn't want to stay with you."

Zara set down her glass before she spilled anything and jerked free of both of them. "I'm not a chew toy," she said. "If you'll excuse me, I would very much like to have a word with my sister."

She turned on her high heel and stalked away. If

Fiona were still alive, she would have winced at Zara's unladylike movements, but desperate times called for expedient behavior, Zara thought. She ducked into the crowd, trying to put as much room between herself and the two pit bulls as she could.

She hated their pretension and their false compliments. Most of all she hated that a week ago, they wouldn't even have acknowledged that she was alive.

"If you're looking for Cleo, she's over there."

Zara realized that Rafe was still next to her, keeping up easily, parting the crowd when necessary. She slowed down.

"That was awful," she said, turning in the direction he'd indicated. "I can't believe how those two acted."

"They find you appealing."

She looked at him. "Oh, please. Somehow they've figured out the truth. They don't care about me. They want a royal connection."

"I'm not sure the duke needs one."

"Then he needs something else."

"They're both rich and eligible."

She stopped and glared at him. "I don't think either of them would appreciate you championing his cause."

"They might if it worked." He moved closer. "So maybe you catch their attention by being Hassan's daughter. Is that so horrible? They might both turn out to be great guys."

She hated that it was so easy for him to imagine her with someone else. Just standing there close to Rafe made her remember what it had been like to kiss

DIANA PALMER

MERCENARY WOMAN
SOLDIERS OF FORTUNE

We'd like to send you **2 FREE** books and a surprise gift to introduce you to Silhouette Special Edition®. Accept our special offer today and

Get Ready for a totally Refreshing Experience!

HOW TO QUALIFY:

1. With a coin, carefully scratch off the silver area on the card at right to see what we have for you—2 FREE BOOKS and a FREE GIFT—ALL YOURS! ALL FREE!

2. Send back the card and you'll receive two brand-new Silhouette Special Edition® novels. These books have a cover price of $4.50 each in the U.S. and $5.25 each in Canada, but they are yours to keep absolutely free!

3. There's no catch. You're under no obligation to buy anything. We charge nothing—ZERO—for your first shipment and you don't have to make any minimum number of purchases—not even one!

4. The fact is, thousands of readers enjoy receiving books by mail from the Silhouette Reader Service®. They enjoy the convenience of home delivery…they like getting the best new novels at discount prices, BEFORE they're available in stores…and they love their *Heart to Heart* subscriber newsletter featuring author news, horoscopes, recipes, book reviews and much more!

5. We hope that after receiving your free books you'll want to remain a subscriber. But the choice is yours—to continue or cancel, any time at all. So why not take us up on our invitation with no risk of any kind. You'll be glad you did!

SPECIAL FREE GIFT!

We can't tell you what it is…but we're sure you'll like it! A FREE gift just for giving the Silhouette Reader Service® a try!

Visit us at
www.eHarlequin.com

The **2 FREE BOOKS** we send you will be selected from **SILHOUETTE SPECIAL EDITION®**, the series that brings you...emotional novels about life, love and creating families.

Books received may vary.

Scratch off the silver area to see what the Silhouette Reader Service has for you.

Silhouette®
Where love comes alive™

YES! I have scratched off the silver area above. Please send me the **2 FREE** books and gift for which I qualify. I understand I am under no obligation to purchase any books, as explained on the back and on the opposite page.

335 SDL DH5C   235 SDL DH5A

FIRST NAME	LAST NAME

ADDRESS

APT.#	CITY

STATE/PROV.	ZIP/POSTAL CODE

Offer limited to one per household and not valid to current Silhouette Special Edition® subscribers. All orders subject to approval.

THE SILHOUETTE READER SERVICE®—Here's how it works:

Accepting your 2 free books and gift places you under no obligation to buy anything. You may keep the books and gift and return the shipping statement marked "cancel." If you do not cancel, about a month later we'll send you 6 additional books and bill you just $3.80 each in the U.S., or $4.21 each in Canada, plus 25¢ shipping & handling per book and applicable taxes if any.* That's the complete price and — compared to cover prices of $4.50 each in the U.S. and $5.25 each in Canada — it's quite a bargain! You may cancel at any time, but if you choose to continue, every month we'll send you 6 more books, which you may either purchase at the discount price or return to us and cancel your subscription.

*Terms and prices subject to change without notice. Sales tax applicable in N.Y. Canadian residents will be charged applicable provincial taxes and GST.

If offer card is missing write to: Silhouette Reader Service, 3010 Walden Ave., P.O. Box 1867, Buffalo NY 14240-1867

DETACH AND MAIL CARD TODAY!

BUSINESS REPLY MAIL
FIRST-CLASS MAIL   PERMIT NO. 717-003   BUFFALO, NY

POSTAGE WILL BE PAID BY ADDRESSEE

SILHOUETTE READER SERVICE
3010 WALDEN AVE
PO BOX 1867
BUFFALO NY 14240-9952

NO POSTAGE
NECESSARY
IF MAILED
IN THE
UNITED STATES

him. It made her want to do it again. Being in his arms had awakened her to a passion she'd never experienced before. Being in his arms had made her feel safe, and that was a commodity that she appreciated now more than ever.

"If you don't understand that it matters to me why they're interested, then I can't explain it."

She turned and headed toward her sister. Cleo was standing very close to one of the princes. Even from twenty feet away Zara could feel the heat flaring between them. At least someone was having a great time tonight.

"Hi," Cleo said when they approached. "You remember Prince Sadik. I guess he's your half brother." She leaned toward the prince. "Which makes the two of us absolutely no relation at all."

Her new half brother bowed. "Zara. I had hoped to have the opportunity to get to know you. Perhaps later you will honor me with a dance?"

Zara nodded. "Sure. No problem."

She waved goodbye and managed to escape without stumbling. When they were out of earshot, she turned to Rafe.

"Dancing?" she hissed. "There's going to be dancing?"

He laughed. "Just you, Jean-Paul and Duke Byron. I can't wait to watch."

Chapter Eight

When Prince Sadik appeared at her side for his dance, Zara nearly wept in relief. She'd just spent a horrible ninety minutes dancing with men she didn't know—mostly Jean-Paul and Byron. Not only were they treating her like a prize desired by a rival, but rather than talking to her while they danced, they spent their time glaring at each other. Maybe they should simply tango together and leave her out of it.

"How are you enjoying yourself?" Prince Sadik asked as he led her around the dance floor.

"It's been lovely," she lied through slightly clenched teeth.

The prince smiled. "Your sister has said you have some reservations about being a part of the family."

Zara sighed. "Don't worry. After I strangle her, she won't be talking at all."

"The information was hardly a revelation," her half brother told her. "This would be a change from almost any life. Of course you are not sure. Our ways are different, our country is strange to you."

Zara stared up into his dark eyes. "Does everyone hate me? I mean I simply showed up out of nowhere, and Hassan is convinced that I'm, well—" she shrugged "—you know."

"The child of his beloved Fiona. Yes, I know." Sadik shook his head. "Do not worry yourself on that account. No one resents your arrival."

He was being polite, she thought. Or maybe he didn't know about Sabrina's unhappy relationship with her father. Men weren't always very observant about that sort of thing.

The dance ended and Sadik excused himself to go find Cleo. Zara watched him hurry away. At least one of them was having fun. She turned and spied Jean-Paul heading in her direction. That meant Byron couldn't be too far away. She ducked around several couples and headed for the stairs on the opposite side of the room. From there she might be able to spot Rafe. For all his claims to want to keep his eye on her, he'd been surprisingly absent since dinner.

She'd just reached the stairs when she felt a hand on her arm. Fearing the worst, she glanced over her shoulder, then sagged in relief when she saw Rafe.

"You abandoned me," she accused.

"I was letting you have a good time."

She exhaled loudly. "A lot you know about women if you think what I've been doing is fun."

"Don't you like dancing?"

"Not with two men acting more like terriers than humans. Plus, aren't they a little old to be sulking?"

Rafe grinned. She liked the lines that formed beside the corners of his eyes and the way his tanned skin contrasted with his short blond hair.

"I saw you dancing with Sadik. That should have been all right."

"It was. He mostly tried to reassure me about my acceptance in the family. I'm not sure I believe him."

"You should." He glanced over her shoulder. "Don't look now, but there are terriers approaching right behind you."

Zara winced. "Rafe, at the risk of sounding too forward, are you allowed to dance with me?"

"Sure."

"Then maybe you should ask."

He did that one better. He swept her up in his arms and moved her into the swirling crowd. Thanks to her mother's training, Zara knew all the basic dance steps. She moved easily to the steady beat of the waltz, stumbling only when she realized how well Rafe was doing.

"I didn't think they taught dancing at paramilitary school," she said breathlessly through a turn.

"I'm a man of many talents."

For several minutes they danced in comfortable silence. She remembered that afternoon, how she'd felt in his arms. It had been different from being in them now, but despite the casual embrace and the people all around them, she felt safe and very feminine. She wanted him.

"Zara."

Her name came out in a growl. The low tone sent shivers dancing along her spine. She raised her chin slightly.

"You feel it, too," she murmured.

"So what? What we feel is irrelevant."

The man was entirely too difficult. "I'm not sure I believe you—about the head cutting, I mean. The king wouldn't really do that to you."

"You have no way of knowing what he would or wouldn't do. I've been around him much longer than you and I'm familiar with the ways of this world."

Maybe it was the tension of the evening that made her so light-headed and bold. Maybe it was the lingering desire and the knowledge that no one had ever made her feel the way Rafe did.

"What about kissing?" she asked in a whisper. "That can't be against the law."

For a second she thought she might have gone too far. Maybe she was making a fool of herself. Then she saw Rafe's eyes darken and a muscle twitch at the corner of his mouth.

"No kissing. It leads to trouble."

"Coward."

His gaze narrowed. "Insulting me isn't going to help."

"I was trying to dare you into acting."

"It didn't work."

"What will?"

The music ended. Rafe stepped away and bowed. "Zara, you tempt me in ways I can't begin to explain. But know this. I will never give in."

She sighed. "That's the most backhanded compliment I've ever heard."

"I meant every word."

Zara escaped into the ladies' room rather than face Byron and Jean-Paul. While she was disappointed that Rafe hadn't jumped on her suggestion that they kiss again, she couldn't stop smiling as she remembered his claim to find her tempting. She didn't think she'd ever tempted a man before—certainly not one like him.

He had seen and done things she couldn't even imagine. No doubt there had been many women along the way. She could imagine him with beautiful, exotic types—of which she was neither. Still, it was nice to know that she could get his attention even for only a minute.

Zara paused in the foyer of the ladies' room and looked around. She'd never been in a bathroom that had a foyer before. The spacious area was decorated in red and gold with an elegant chandelier hanging from the center of the ceiling. Mirrors covered two walls, stretching down to long vanities. A half dozen tufted stools stood ready, offering a seat to those who wished to repair their appearance. The lighting was intensely flattering and there were trays of hair spray, lotion, tissues and small towels to please even the most demanding guest.

"Not bad work if you can get it," Zara murmured to herself. She wandered closer to the mirror and studied her appearance. Her bronze-colored dress shimmered in the light. Her hairstyle by Eric had stayed in place. Her lipstick was a little smudged, and there was a dark blotch of mascara just under the corner of her right eye. After sinking onto one of the stools, she wiped away the smudge and dark spot, then reapplied her lipstick. Getting off her feet felt heavenly. She wasn't used to high heels, not to mention strappy sandal styles. The thin bits of leather looked great but they cut into her feet.

The main door opened. Zara looked up, then stiffened when she saw Sabrina enter. Her half sister wore a dress of pale gold. The fabric emphasized Sabrina's curvy shape. No padding required, Zara thought glumly.

Cool dark eyes regarded her thoughtfully. Sabrina smiled—it looked a little forced to Zara—then sat gracefully two stools away.

"Are you enjoying yourself?" Sabrina asked as she opened her small handbag and drew out a lip pencil.

"Everything is lovely." Zara pressed her hands together in her lap. "I spoke with Prince Sadik earlier and he was very kind."

Sabrina finished lining her lips and smiled again. "I doubt he would appreciate the description. My brothers are more interested in being ruthless and arrogant."

"Oh."

Zara didn't know what to say to that. She felt tense and out of place. Rafe's story about why Sabrina didn't like her swirled through her head. She hated knowing her only sister by blood resented her being here.

Zara drew in a deep breath and turned to face Sabrina. "I'm sorry about all of this. For invading your life the way I have. I didn't think that coming here would make trouble, which was naive of me. I should have seen the potential problems."

Sabrina carefully applied lipstick, then blotted her mouth with a tissue. Finally she put her cosmetics back in her purse and closed it. Only then did she look at Zara.

"Your apology makes me think that you've been told something of my past."

Zara nodded. "Rafe mentioned a few things."

Sabrina sighed. "I know this isn't your fault. Intellectually I understand that my father's delight in having you show up doesn't take away anything from my relationship with him. But my heart tells me something else. I spent my childhood being in the way both with my mother in California and here in Bahania with Father. It's difficult to watch him dance with joy when he sees you."

Zara hung her head. She felt like slime. "I'm sorry," she murmured.

"Don't be. Like I said, it's not your fault. For that matter it's not my fault, either. My father has come to see that he treated me badly and he's trying to make amends. I have reconciled to the fact that I'll never be his favorite. While I was able to convince myself it was because I was female, I could handle it quite well."

Zara winced. Hassan hadn't cared that she was a girl. He'd been thrilled just to see Fiona's child, regardless of gender. For Sabrina that would be rubbing salt in the wound.

"I don't know what to say," she admitted.

Sabrina smiled. "You don't have to say anything. This isn't your responsibility. You came here because you wanted to find something."

"Roots," Zara admitted. "All my life I've wanted to know about my father. My mom wouldn't ever talk about him." She glanced around the foyer and smiled slightly. "But in all my dreams, I never once imagined something like this."

Sabrina laughed. "Bahania would be tough to make up. It's so incredible all on its own."

"I agree."

There was a moment of awkward silence. Zara cleared her throat. "Thanks for sending Marie with the dresses. She was great."

"I thought that would be better than my castoffs. Plus, Cleo wouldn't have fit in any of my things."

Zara looked at her half sister. "Not to mention you not wanting us to wear your clothes."

Sabrina shrugged. "I'm big enough to admit that would have bugged me. But speaking of clothes, Marie left me a message saying that you and Cleo only picked out dresses for tonight. Why not a whole wardrobe?"

"That wouldn't be right. We're not here for what we can get. I don't want anyone to think I'm in it for the money. Neither of us had a dress appropriate for tonight, and frankly we couldn't afford anything from Marie's boutique. So we had to accept these, but that's enough."

Sabrina regarded her thoughtfully. "I think I believe you."

"I can't make you believe me or not. I'm simply telling the truth."

"Regardless of what you want in terms of gifts, you're going to need an appropriate wardrobe. Unless you were married to the president in your previous life, I doubt you'll have much that works. I'll send Marie back in the morning. Take her advice. Enjoy the clothes. Think of them as a welcoming gift."

Zara wasn't sure what to make of Sabrina's words. She hated that she and her half sister were at odds. If only there was a way to make things right. Unfortunately, the past was over, and there wasn't a way to change it.

Sabrina rose to her feet. "I'm not a horrible person," she announced. "You're looking at me as if I'm about to slap you."

Zara stood, as well. "That's not what I'm thinking at all. You've been very patient."

Sabrina shook her head. "No. I've been pouting. Ask my husband." She took a step closer. "Let's start over and try to be friends. I have to admit that after having four brothers for so many years, not to mention being the youngest, I wouldn't mind having another woman in the family. We're sisters. We need to stick together."

Tension eased in Zara's chest. She smiled. "I'd like that."

Sabrina held out her arms and they embraced. Behind them the bathroom door opened. Zara stepped back and turned to see who had entered, but no one was there. She returned her attention to Sabrina.

"Would you mind if we spoke in the next day or

so? I have so many questions and I don't know who
to ask.''

''Not a problem,'' Sabrina promised. ''We'll get to
know each other.''

Hassan claimed Zara for the last dance of the evening. Zara had tried to escape back to her room twice
before, but Rafe had intercepted and sent her back
into the crowd, telling her that no member of the royal
family was allowed to duck out before the king.

Now she found herself glad she had stayed. Hassan
was a very charming man.

''You must see all of Bahania,'' he was saying as
they moved around the dance floor. ''Not all in one
day, of course.''

She laughed. ''I did some research before I left.
From what I could tell, your country has much di-
versity.''

''Ah, but it is *your* country, too, now,'' he reminded her. ''I will instruct Rafe to take you exploring.''

She felt a whisper of anticipation. ''I'd like that.''
Not only seeing the splendors of Bahania, but spending time with her temporary bodyguard.

''I will introduce you to my favorite cats,'' he continued. ''I'm sure you've noticed all the cats around
the palace.''

''Of course. They're everywhere.''

''They are my pride and joy.'' He squeezed her
hand, his dark eyes bright with laughter. ''Until you
arrived.''

She wasn't sure how she felt about displacing a cat

or two in his affections. No wonder Sabrina had been miffed at her arrival. Sabrina had probably come a distant third to Hassan's sons and his cats.

"We have much to make up for," Hassan said.

"I agree. Although I have to admit that all the times I stayed awake as a little girl and fantasized about finding my real father, I never pictured anything like this."

His humor faded. "How I wish I'd known about you. I would have come and swept you away." He paused. "Or perhaps I would have simply watched from afar. I do not think I could have hurt Fiona by taking away her child. But then I doubt I could have kept from wanting her to be mine forever, so I might have had you both eventually. We'll never know."

Zara didn't know what to say to that. She was tired and fading fast. Late-night parties weren't a part of her usual world.

"Speaking of true love," her father said. "I saw you spent much of your time with two particular gentlemen. Both Byron and Jean-Paul would make fine matches."

Zara suddenly felt as if she'd fallen into the pages of a Jane Austen novel. "I'm not really looking for a 'fine match,'" she told him honestly. "Right now I have plenty of changes to keep me occupied."

"For a time, but eventually you will want more. A husband, perhaps? A family?"

They were all Zara had ever wanted. Roots, she thought longingly. "I've thought of those things," she admitted.

"Then you should spend time with Byron and

Jean-Paul. Get to know them. I know they will be charmed by you. Something may light a spark.''

She'd already been set on fire and it hadn't been by either man in question. Unfortunately, the king wasn't offering Rafe as a potential bridegroom. Too bad. That would have been a whole lot easier to take. Still, she couldn't bring herself to dim the light of hope in his eyes.

''I promise to give them a chance, if they decide they would like to see me again.''

''Of course they will want to see you,'' Hassan promised in a tone that warned her he would make sure it happened.

Zara had a moment of longing for her small, normal life back in Washington. Somehow she knew that things were never going to be the same again.

Rafe carried Zara's shoes as he escorted her back to her room. She walked gingerly, wincing as she stepped on a bit of uneven tile.

''Remind me to pick low-heeled shoes next time,'' she said, pausing to bend over and rub the ball of her left foot. ''I think I broke something tonight.''

''You'll feel better in the morning,'' he promised.

''Only if someone carries me around so I don't have to walk.''

He had an instant picture of himself carrying her. The image wasn't unpleasant—in fact, he found himself warming to the idea. The only problem was carrying Zara anywhere would ultimately end up with him carrying her to bed. And as much as she might enjoy teasing him about kissing, she had no idea of the consequences of those actions. Which meant he was going to keep his mind firmly on business.

"Did you have a good time?" he asked as they reached a T intersection in the hallway. Zara turned right, forcing him to stop her and point to the left.

"It was interesting," she said and stifled a yawn. "I have to tell you that I don't think I'm the state dinner type. I tried not to say anything too awful or offend anyone, but saying or doing the wrong thing seems incredibly easy. With my ability to put my foot in my mouth, I should be kept away from sensitive situations."

"You did fine."

She looked at him and raised her eyebrows. "Do you really think the terrier twins were paying attention to what I was saying?"

Fatigue left dark shadows under her eyes. Her skin was pale, her mouth free of lipstick. He thought she looked lovely.

"I'm sure that Byron and Jean-Paul were charmed by you."

She wrinkled her nose. "Yeah, right. The worst part is the king wants me to see them again. I think he's hoping for a match."

Rafe felt an instant tightness in his chest. He told himself that Zara seeing any man wasn't his business. His responsibilities lay in keeping her safe, not escorting her around town. She was the kind of woman who needed to be married; he was the kind of man who did best on his own. End of story.

"What are *you* hoping for?" he asked.

"I don't know. Answers, mostly. Is Hassan my father? Do I belong here? Actually I have the answer to the last question. I don't belong here and I'm not sure I ever will.'' She paused and glanced around to make sure they were alone. ''Can you keep a secret?''

''Yes. Although if this is about something that involves your safety, I have to warn you that I may tell the king.''

She pressed her lips together. ''Don't you ever go off duty?''

''No.''

She sighed. ''This doesn't affect my safety. I just wish—'' She leaned against the tiled wall and closed her eyes. ''Sometimes I wish I hadn't come here. That I didn't know the truth. Although the blood test might show that I'm not Hassan's daughter.''

''Don't count on it.''

''I know.''

Rafe studied her pale face. His fingers itched to trace her pretty features. He wanted to pull her close and kiss her, running his hands up and down her body. He wanted to feel her delicate curves, touch her bare skin and taste every inch of her.

The erotic fantasy produced predictable results. Rafe swore silently as blood rushed to his groin, hardening him in an instant.

''Come on,'' he said, taking Zara by the hand and gently tugging her down the hall. ''It's time for princesses to be in bed.''

''Are you tucking me in?'' she asked playfully.

''Not in this lifetime.''

They stopped in front of her door. She looked at him. ''You know, it's strange. In my regular life I would never come on to any guy, and if I did, any hint of rejection would leave me devastated for the rest of my life. Yet here I'm very comfortable begging you for the smallest of favors and despite your constant refusal, I survive."

"You're tough."

She shook her head. "I think it's because every time I mention something illicit, your eyes darken with fire. I like the heat."

Desire poured through him. Rafe would have sold his soul that second if he could have hauled Zara up against him and taken her. He ached to fill her with his arousal, to teach her exactly what kind of magic went on between men and women.

"You're imagining it," he said instead.

"Nope. Not even for a second. Oh, I almost forgot to tell you that Byron invited me to go horseback riding with him in two days. Apparently, it gets really hot in the afternoon so we'll be heading out early. I hope that's all right with you."

It was as if she'd slapped him. Rafe felt the sting, but didn't allow himself to show any kind of reaction. Her personal affairs didn't matter, he reminded himself. This assignment was temporary. Soon he would be back in the City of Thieves, and Zara Paxton would be little more than a memory.

"Just let me know when and where," he told her. "I'll be there."

"Armed?" she asked teasingly.

"Always."

Her smile faded. "Tell me you want to kiss me good-night, Rafe. I think I've earned that."

Involuntarily he dropped his gaze to her mouth. He remembered her taste, the sweet intake of her breath when he'd stroked her tongue. Oh, yeah, he wanted to kiss her.

"You're making my life hell, Zara. Is that good enough?"

She raised herself up on tiptoes and lightly kissed his cheek. "Almost," she told him, before taking her shoes from him and slipping into her room.

This was so not what she'd planned, Zara thought two days later as she rode across the desert. Somehow in her mind the experience had become a cross between a scene in a movie and a perfume commercial. She'd imagined dew glistening on the lush foliage, the sun rising in the east, herself riding elegantly next to a handsome man as their horses galloped across the rolling hills of the desert.

To begin with it was darned hot, even a few minutes before sunrise. Second, lush foliage didn't fit into the desert and any dew had long been sucked up by the dry, heated air. Last but certainly not least, her half a dozen experiences on tired rental horses at a local stable had not prepared her for the reality of trying to stay on a purebred Arabian gelding.

"How are you doing?" Byron asked.

"Great," she lied, flopping more out than in the saddle.

At least Byron looked the part...sort of, she thought. He rode well and appeared halfway decent in his riding clothes. It wasn't his fault that she found Rafe far more compelling. Even though the men had similar coloring, there was no comparing their builds or faces. Rafe was the hands-down winner.

"It's a beautiful morning," Byron called out as her horse drifted to the left.

"Yes, beautiful."

She tried to ease her mount back into line. The horse didn't want to cooperate. Obviously, the stable guy had been having a laugh at her expense when he'd promised a gentle horse. That or there weren't any gentle, easy, *slow* horses in Bahania. Thank goodness they'd stopped trotting and were now walking. At least her butt wasn't forever slapping against the hard leather of the saddle. While she knew she was going to be sore later, she couldn't help feeling sorry for the horse. She doubted the creature appreciated being pounded by her bony butt.

"Are you…"

The rest of Byron's sentence was drowned out by the powerful engines behind him. Zara tried to glance over her shoulder, but the movement made her slip more than she could handle and she had to grab on to the horse's mane to stay in the saddle. Still, she didn't have to see the three Hummers and two Jeeps, all filled with armed guards to know they were there.

Instead she turned to glare at Rafe, who rode easily, just a few paces behind them. The man was making her crazy. A bodyguard she could accept. A bodyguard who obviously enjoyed tormenting her was a pain, but also doable. But when he insisted on mocking her, that was too much to stand.

The amount of security he'd arranged for the ride was insane. Every time she and Byron tried to speak, the vehicles drew closer, making it impossible to hear what the other person was saying.

Zara reined in her horse. The animal stopped, which surprised her. Byron slowed his horse. Behind him the motorcade drew to a halt.

"What is it?" Byron asked.

Nothing about the man appealed to her, yet she had told the king she would give Byron a chance. So here she was—keeping her word.

"I thought if we stopped moving, they might stop getting so close," she told him. "I'm sorry this all turned out so badly."

He moved his horse closer. "Your father wants to keep you safe."

Zara held in a groan. The fact that Byron knew or had guessed her relationship with the king shouldn't be a surprise. Still she felt disappointed. Telling herself no one would be interested in her for herself was one thing, but having it highlighted was another.

Rafe rode to her other side. "Is everything all right?"

"Yes. The duke and I are having a conversation."

He had the audacity to grin and ask, "What about?"

Chapter Nine

Zara stalked out of the stable without saying anything. Rafe had been in the middle of telling the horse trainer that none of the mounts had been pushed very hard when he was forced to break off in midsentence to go after her. The stiffness of her walk and the set of her head warned him that she was furious.

Rafe acknowledged that he'd probably gone a bit too far with the Hummers and the Jeeps. Not to mention the armed guards. The odds of a kidnapping taking place were slim at best. Hardly anyone knew about her. Word would spread quickly, but right now she was fairly safe. Still, he'd been unable to resist calling in the troops—to give the duke something to think about if nothing else.

However, Zara hadn't seen things that way. Worse, she'd probably hated having an audience while she struggled to stay on her horse. Obviously, she hadn't had much practice riding horses bred in a royal stable.

"Zara, wait."

He caught up with her in the courtyard between the stable and the house. The sun had already drifted well into the sky, and the heat sucked the air from his lungs. They stood in the shade of a cluster of date palms, but the temperature still had to be over a hundred degrees.

She spun to face him, temper flaring in her brown eyes. "What do you want?" she demanded as she pushed up her glasses. "I would think you've already had your joke for the day."

He instantly felt like a jerk. "I'm sorry," he told her. "I guess I went a little too far."

"Yes, you did."

She drew in a breath, then sank down on the blanket of grass by the trees. After drawing her legs to her chest she rested her forehead on her knees.

They were in a small grove of palms, protected from view by the foliage at the base of the trees. Except for a cat grooming in the sun a few feet away, they were alone.

"It's not you," she mumbled. "I'm angry at Byron."

Rafe crouched next to her. He wasn't concerned that Byron had tried anything—he hadn't left them alone long enough for anything to happen. "What did he do?"

"Nothing. It's what he said." She raised her head and glared at him. "Do I look stupid to you?"

"Not at all."

"I didn't think so. Men worrying that I'm not smart enough has never been the problem. Usually they think I'm too smart."

"So the duke thought you were an idiot?"

"Apparently." She rubbed her temples. "I can't even say it. It's just too humiliating."

Rafe rose to his feet. "If he insulted you—"

"He did, but not the way you're thinking," she said, interrupting. She looked away. "He said I was beautiful."

"What?" Rafe frowned. That was hardly an insult. He ignored the tension in his chest that told him he didn't like the duke complimenting Zara.

"You heard me."

He sank next to her on the grass. She wore her hair down in a thick braid. As she spoke, she twisted the braid around her fingers.

"Why is that so horrible?" he asked. "Don't you want him saying nice things?"

She rolled her eyes. "I don't want him lying to me and expecting me to believe him. I would have accepted pretty or even attractive. But beautiful? The man obviously thinks I'm a moron. Or he doesn't think at all. Or he assumes that I'll be so bowled over by his flattery that I won't bother to question his sincerity."

"I think you're making too much of this."

"Of course you'd say that. You're a man. But it's significant to me."

Rafe sensed he was treading on dangerous territory. He decided to go slowly and carefully. "You're an attractive woman, Zara. Beauty isn't universal. Maybe

Byron was telling the truth from his point of view, but you don't feel comfortable admitting it.'' He hated that he was defending the guy.

"Maybe camels fly here in the desert.'' She glared at him. "I understand how all this works. When people meet there's either an attraction or there isn't. That attraction can color someone's view but it's not going to take it out of the realm of reality. I mean you have obviously had sexual feelings for me, at least that one time when we kissed, yet you'd never say I was beautiful.''

She paused just long enough to make Rafe sweat. There was a deep, dark conversation pit right in front of him and he didn't know how to keep from falling in. Fortunately Zara kept talking.

"If Byron knew me and had spent time with me, I just might believe him. But right now he's just playing some stupid game with me and it's really annoying. Is it always going to be like this? I thought getting a date was bad before, but this is impossible.''

Another of the king's cats strolled by. Rafe patted the creature before turning his attention back to Zara.

"Take a deep breath and slow down,'' he told her. "First of all, you're still getting used to a new situation. It won't always be so confusing. Second, give yourself some credit. You act like you're the female version of the elephant man. That's not true.''

"I know the kind of woman I am, and I know what men say about me.'' She tossed her braid back over her shoulder. "I'm smart and intimidating. Not beautiful, not sexy. Cleo's the man magnet in this family.''

"You're not giving yourself enough credit.'' He

found her damned sexy, although he couldn't tell her. Not without creating a different kind of trouble.

She shook her head impatiently. "Get real. My dissertation was on the changing face of society as demonstrated by feminist writers in the last quarter of the twentieth century. I doubt that makes you think of sweaty sheets. It's just impossible. I'm never going to find someone who wants me."

She'd gone from angry to vulnerable in a heartbeat. He could handle the former, but not the latter. Her slumped shoulders and bleak expression made him want to pull her close and offer comfort. A dangerous proposition, he reminded himself. He was the hired help—nothing more.

"You'll find him," he told her. "The right guy is out there."

"How will I find him? And where is he? If you have any names with you, please feel free to pass them along."

She started to get to her feet. Involuntarily Rafe grabbed her wrist to hold her in place. The second his fingers touched her soft skin, he knew he'd made a really big mistake. Especially when she looked at him and he saw the questions in her big eyes. Questions and desire.

An answering spark leaped to life inside of him. His self-control deserted him, leaving him hungry. There was only one way to satisfy his appetite. Only one way and with one woman...

"Rafe."

She breathed his name, the single syllable giving away more than she realized. He heard the anticipation, the wanting. It increased the fire inside of him, burning away the last of his resistance. Before he could come to his senses and head for the open desert, he pulled her close.

She melted against him. Her arms came around his neck as he hauled her onto his lap. He shifted so that he could lean against the base of a date palm. The right side of her chest pressed against his. She was hot, sweet and more desirable than any woman he'd ever known. At that moment he felt as if he would die if he didn't kiss her.

So he did. He moved his lips against hers, exploring what he'd discovered before, listening for the sound of her breath catching, pleased when her fingers trembled. He licked her lower lip. When she parted, he slipped inside, teasing her, tasting her, taking her deeply, insistently. She didn't shy away or protest. Instead she strained toward him, circling his tongue, then closing her lips around him and sucking gently.

Need shot to his groin, engorging him to the point of discomfort. He swore silently, knowing this was a game he couldn't win. Not with her.

But she tempted him beyond reason. One of his hands lay on her thigh. He moved his palm along the outside seam of her slacks to the curve of her hip. From there he slipped to her rear. He squeezed the roundness, then eased her into a straddling position with her feminine center resting directly on his need.

It was an unbearable combination of pleasure and pain. He couldn't help grabbing her hips and rocking her against him. Her body moved easily as they found a rhythm that made them both gasp. She cupped his face and continued to kiss him. Tension made her shudder. He could feel her arousal growing, not to mention his own. The second he began calculating the distance to a more private location, he knew he'd crossed the line. He grabbed her around the waist and lifted her off.

Zara was caught by surprise. She flashed him a hurt look. "You can't be stopping now."

"I have to."

He stood up and turned his back on her. He ached with desire. Every inch of him throbbed in time with his rapid heartbeat. What the hell was wrong with him? He never allowed himself to get pulled off course during an assignment. In other circumstances, this sort of distraction could get him killed. He knew better.

"I'm sorry," he ground out. "I shouldn't have done that."

He sensed her moving and turned to see her scrambling to her feet.

"Don't make it worse by apologizing," she muttered. "I don't understand what the big deal is. There's obviously a huge attraction between us. No one has to know that we explored it."

"It's not that simple. I have a responsibility to protect you, even from yourself. And if that's not a good enough reason, then try telling yourself that these sorts of things have a life of their own. Do you really want to read about your personal life in the tabloids?"

"That would never happen."

He didn't bother responding. Zara was new to this

world, but he wasn't. He'd seen the disastrous consequence of an ill-timed affair.

"You're making me crabby," she told him. "I hate being crabby. Not to mention confused. I want things with you I've never wanted with anyone else. Worse, I'm telling you that and even acting on the impulses. This is so not me. What's going on here? Is it being in Bahania. Is it the water or maybe early signs of senility?"

Rafe didn't have an answer. Or maybe he didn't want to see the truth. He and Zara generated a lot of attraction between them. The heat was dangerous to both of them.

She put her hands on her hips. "Should I assume your silence means you don't have an answer, either?"

"Not one that makes sense."

"How helpful is that?" She sighed. "Everything about this situation is unfamiliar. I've actually teased you about kissing me. I never do that."

"I never let personal interfere with business."

She stared at him. "So this isn't usual for you?"

"Not even close."

A smile curved up the corners of her mouth. "That makes me feel a little better."

He didn't respond to that statement. There was no point in telling her that his inability to ignore the passion between them had him wondering what the hell was wrong with him. When had he gotten so damn soft? He needed a few weeks in a war zone to improve his reflexes and his self-control.

"Where do we go from here?" Zara asked.

"Nowhere. Nothing's changed. I work for the king and I don't get involved with his daughter."

She dropped her arms to her sides. "You need to find some new material," she told him. "This same story is getting old." She turned on her heel and headed for the palace, then paused.

"Oh, by the way, Jean-Paul has invited me to dinner and I accepted. I think you'll need to dress formally."

Rafe watched her go, her head high, her slender hips swaying gently. She was back in a temper. She'd also had the last word. Princess Zara…formally Zara Paxton, professor, was turning out to be more trouble than he'd imagined possible. And damned if he didn't like every second of it.

Once she reached the palace, Zara headed for her room. Dozens of thoughts swirled through her brain, and she didn't know what was going on. Life had certainly taken a turn for the interesting ever since she'd landed in Bahania. She'd been prepared to feel conflicted about meeting the stranger who might be her father, but she'd never thought she could have man trouble.

For the first time in her life she had two men vying for her attention. Of course neither of them really cared about her—they were interested in getting a connection with the royal family. Of course, there might be a different motive—maybe the duke needed money for his aging manor house. Or Jean-Paul might want a loan to expand the vineyard. Whatever their reasons for pursuing her, she knew they had nothing to do with her as a person. So while her popularity was a change, it was especially unappealing.

She turned the corner and headed for the door leading to the rooms she shared with Cleo. As she stepped inside, she called her sister's name, but heard only silence. Cleo must be out—maybe with the fabulously handsome Prince Sadik. He had certainly taken notice of Cleo at the state dinner.

Zara wandered around the spacious living room, then plopped down on the sofa. She could see the Arabian Sea in the distance. Already the sun was high in the sky. The temperature would be climbing, and soon it would be difficult for her to be out in the heat. But here in the palace the air was cool.

Zara glanced around at the elegant furnishings, the expensive tapestries and the small wet bar in the corner. She knew if she crossed to it and opened the minirefrigerator, she would find an assortment of drinks, including her favorite sodas. The small cupboard above held different snacks. She could even phone the kitchen and ask that something be sent up.

Bahania was a fantasy come true for her. In fact it was better than her fantasy. She was living in a palace, and if King Hassan really did turn out to be her father, then she was about to become a princess. So what if that made a couple of guys a little weird?

Zara rose and walked to the floor-to-ceiling windows. Restlessness filled her and she knew the cause. Rafe. She didn't understand anything about him.

She also knew that she was playing a very dangerous game with him. She'd learned a few things in the twenty-eight years she'd spent on the planet, and one of them was that men didn't lie about certain things. When a guy said he didn't do relationships, she needed to listen. The problem was, she didn't want to.

Zara sighed. Rafe had told her that she was a marriage-and-kids kind of woman and that he wasn't a marriage-and-kids kind of guy. Her gut told her that he was telling the truth on both counts. Unfortunately, knowing he was a mistake didn't take away his appeal.

She wanted him.

Some of the attraction was sexual. He made her think about things she'd never considered. For the first time in her life she was responding to a man based on chemistry. But there was more to it than that. She couldn't dismiss everything as being due to hormones.

She liked him.

Zara put her fingertips on the cool glass. She wished it was otherwise, but wishing didn't change things. She liked being with him, talking with him. She even liked it when they argued. He was straightforward and so masculine. He was kind, although she suspected he would hate that description. He was also attracted to her.

She couldn't remember the last time a man had been interested in her body with the same intensity Rafe showed. She could see his desire, as well as feel it. How was she supposed to resist that? The combination of sexual attraction and general liking weren't a temptation she could walk away from. Around him she felt safe and yet strong. She'd never experienced that particular combination before.

She had it bad for the man, but somehow she was going to have to find a way to get over him. No way was she going to allow herself to get her heart broken.

"This is the sword an ancestor of mine carried during the Crusades," King Hassan said when they paused in front of a long, dangerous-looking sword on a stand. Jewels and gold decorated the handle, but their beauty didn't detract from the honed edge of the blade.

Hassan gently touched the tip. "During some battles, blood ran like a river through the valleys of the Holy Land."

Zara stared at the antique weapon. She could imagine it covered in blood. "I didn't realize that Bahania had been involved in the Crusades."

Hassan shook his head. "There wasn't any fighting here, but the true believers traveled to keep out the infidels." His expression turned serious. "It was a time of great unrest, and many died. Over the years, the royal family began to see that an attitude of tolerance was better for our people. By the sixteenth century, all were allowed to worship as each saw fit. We were very progressive."

"Apparently." Zara knew that in the sixteenth century, Europe had been a land of intolerance, especially between those of different beliefs.

"We were less progressive about women," Hassan said with an apologetic tone. "The royal harem existed until my father's time."

"I can't imagine such a thing."

"While I can imagine it, I'm not sure how a ruling monarch would find the time," Hassan said teasingly. "Matters of state keep me very occupied."

They continued to walk through the halls of the oldest part of the palace. Treasures filled every corner, including paintings, stunning mosaics, statues and carvings done directly into the walls and ceilings.

A small gray cat strolled up to join them. Hassan bent over and picked up the feline, cradling it in his arms.

"How are you, my precious one?" he asked, his tone low and affectionate.

A small tag hung from a braided collar. Hassan touched the tag with his finger, turning it so he could read the name.

"Ah. You are Muffin." He shook his head. "Occasionally I permit school children to come to the palace and name the new cats. I frequently regret the visits."

Zara laughed. "You don't approve of Muffin as a name for a cat?"

"Not a royal one." Still, he scratched the cat's head and rubbed it under the chin. The tame creature purred, relaxing in Hassan's arms.

"How did you come to be so fond of cats?" she asked.

"My mother enjoyed having them around." He set Muffin back on the ground. "You are named for my mother. Did you know?"

"Not until you told me. I'd looked up the origin of the name once and saw that it was a derivation of

Sara but I didn't think anything more than that. I figured my mother had simply liked the name.''

Hassan led the way to an alcove. Large windows looked out onto an elaborate garden. Zara had noticed that Bahania was much more lush than she would have expected.

She took the seat next to the king and tried to ignore the small group that had trailed them throughout the tour. Apparently Hassan didn't go many places alone.

''I was surprised to learn that Fiona had remembered me telling her about my mother.'' He touched Zara's hair. ''Surprised and pleased. My mother also would have enjoyed knowing she had not been forgotten.''

Zara didn't know what to say to that. Fiona had never spoken of Hassan or his mother. The king seemed to read her mind.

''If you only learned about me through her papers, obviously she did not tell you anything.''

''I would ask questions,'' Zara said, because it was true and she sensed it was something Hassan would want to hear. ''I used to beg her to tell me about my father, but she never said a word. I didn't know why.''

''Your life would have been very different if she'd told either of us,'' Hassan said. ''I want to think I would have been willing to let her live her life without me as was her wish, but I'm not sure.''

He stared into the distance. Zara knew he was seeing the past he'd shared with Fiona.

"Tell me about your life as a child," he said quietly. "Tell me about Fiona."

Zara shifted slightly on the bench. Even though the king's entourage stayed out of earshot, she was aware of them lurking. There were a couple of assistants, someone who could only be a bodyguard and Rafe. His was the only presence she didn't mind.

"Fiona was always beautiful," Zara began slowly. "Tall, elegant and so graceful. She could make the most ordinary task in the world look like an intricate dance. I wanted to be like her."

"There is a great likeness," Hassan said.

She laughed. "You danced with me at the dinner. I'm sure I trod on your toes at least once." Zara's smile faded slightly. "I inherited many good qualities from my mother, but grace wasn't one of them. I had no talent for dancing, although she tried for years. I would attend classes and stumble my way through. Finally she gave in to my pleas and allowed me to spend my afternoons in the library instead of in her studio."

"Was there—" Hassan's voice trailed off. He cleared his throat. "Fiona had a way about her. There must have been many men. Before you said there wasn't anyone special, but she must have had admirers."

Zara suddenly sensed dangerous territory. Fortunately, she could tell the truth. "From time to time she dated. A relationship might last for a couple of months. But they were never serious. She told me that she had no interest in getting married. I think she'd already given away her heart."

Hassan shrugged. "I want it to be so. How could I not? Fiona was my one true love. If only she'd agreed to marry me."

Zara found that thought daunting. If her mother had married the king, then they all would have lived in Bahania. What would that have been like?

She thought of Sabrina's years growing up, both here and in California. Torn between two worlds. Would Zara have experienced the same fate? And what about Cleo?

"Imagining a different life is difficult," she admitted. "Fiona was telling you the truth when she said that she couldn't live in one place for very long. We moved nearly every year. I never knew what she was looking for, but she didn't find it. Or perhaps there was no goal, and the point was simply to experience different lives."

"We will never know." Hassan patted her hand. "I have a matter I wish to discuss with you, my daughter."

His tone of voice sent warning signals zipping along her spine. Yet she found herself caught up in the words "my daughter." His daughter? Had she really found her father? Despite the week she'd been in the palace, the concept was still difficult to believe.

"Your Highness," she said, not realizing she was interrupting him until it was too late and he was already staring at her. "What about the blood tests? Shouldn't we take care of that. I mean, so that we can be sure?"

"I am sure."

"Yes, well, this isn't just about us. Your family

will want to be sure. The government of Bahania will want to be sure. Your, ah, people will have questions.''

His people? She couldn't believe she'd actually said that. She felt like a bit player in a bad movie.

''My people trust me,'' Hassan intoned.

''With reason, I'm sure. My point is why *ask* them to trust you on this matter? Why not let them know for sure?''

The king considered her words, then nodded. ''I'll send my physician to you later today. He'll draw blood and the appropriate tests will be performed. Does that satisfy you?''

''Yes. Thanks.''

She swallowed. Satisfied didn't exactly describe the sudden roiling of her stomach. While she knew that confirming her relationship—or lack thereof— with the king was the right thing to do, a part of her didn't want to know. The voice deep down in her innermost soul had already whispered the truth. Zara didn't doubt what the blood tests would reveal, and when the truth came out there was no turning back. Her life would be changed forever.

''Good. Now, I have also been considering your future. Once the blood tests have proven what we both already know—that you are my blood—then you will be known to all as my daughter.'' He hesitated. ''Sabrina frequently chides me for how I say things. She tells me that daughters are different from sons and require different persuading.''

Zara had no idea what he was taking about, but he

was making her nervous. "Just say it. I'll try not to be offended."

"Perhaps that would be best." Hassan beamed. "I would be most happy to find you a husband. I mean no disrespect, but you are very advanced in years not to be married. Of course your lack of a husband makes some things less complicated, so I am not displeased. If it has been a matter of finding the right man, I can offer several suggestions."

Zara opened her mouth, then closed it. She couldn't breathe and she certainly couldn't speak. Suggestions? As in he thought he could find her a husband?

She reminded herself that he was the king of Bahania. No doubt he could do whatever he wanted.

"I, ah, feel confident that I can find my own husband," she said at last, the words trembling slightly.

"You have not done so yet."

"I know. It's complicated." No way was she going to tell him about Jon and the broken engagement. And even though she'd told Rafe about her gay ex-fiancé, she didn't think he would be telling her secrets to anyone—not even the king.

"Now that you are in Bahania, you will meet different men. Didn't you go riding with the duke of Netherton?"

"Uh-huh." And it had been a disaster. "I'm not exactly looking for a duke," she told the king. "There's also the issue of me returning home. What would I do with a husband then?"

Hassan stared at her. "You are home."

Her stomach flopped over again. "What do you mean?"

He cupped her cheek. "You are my daughter. You belong here—in Bahania. The palace is your home now. You will stay here until you are married. That is the way of things for the daughter of the king."

He squeezed gently, then released her. Before she could get her lips around a response, he was gone, leaving her gasping, confused and feeling very trapped.

Chapter Ten

"I can't believe he's serious," Zara said as she walked back toward her room. "Does he really expect me to stay in the palace until I'm married? I have a life, a job, a home."

"I guess the king doesn't see it that way."

Rafe held in a chuckle. He didn't think that Zara would appreciate his humor. Not when he could practically see the steam coming out of her ears.

"Have you noticed how you spend a lot of your day annoyed?" he asked conversationally. "Didn't we already do the huffy thing after your ride with Byron?"

She stopped and glared at him. "I wasn't in a huff then and I'm not in one now. It's very easy for you to make fun of me. You're not the one about to be held prisoner in the palace."

Rafe glanced around at the mosaics on the wall, the two cats strolling past and the antique table next to them.

"It's a little hard to get worked up about your living conditions."

She pressed her lips together. "Don't be cute. You know what I mean. I have an entire life. The king thinks I should just drop it and become his...his—" she exhaled "—I don't know the right word. His something."

"Daughter," Rafe offered helpfully. "He wants you to be his daughter. You know, hang out with him, get to know him, live in his country."

"I have a career. I worked hard to get my doctorate. I have friends, plans. Should I just turn my back on everything?"

"I don't know. How great are things back in your world?"

She looked away from him, which Rafe guessed was her way of dealing with the situation in a mature fashion. He prodded the small of her back to get her moving again.

"I sort of understand," he told her. "This whole royal situation takes getting used to."

She sniffed. "A lot you know about it. You get to come and go as you please. You can quit your job anytime you want."

She had a point. The thing was, he kind of liked her all fussy and crabby. She had a temper, but not an ugly one.

"Think of the possibilities," he told her. "You

might start to like it here. You'll get to go shopping, wear jewelry, hang out in the best places.''

''I'm not even going to dignify that with a response,'' she muttered. ''You can't possibly think I'm so incredibly shallow. It's disgusting.''

''Well then, think about all the marriage possibilities. I'm sure Hassan would find you a terrific husband.''

She stopped again and glared at him. ''Ha-ha. I'm nearly doubled over with laughter. Aren't you the amusing one?''

He held back a smile. ''Absolutely.''

She planted her hands on her hips. ''You're not taking this very seriously. I'm talking about the entire fabric of my life being ripped apart and sewn back together without my say-so. I do *not* want anyone picking my husband, thank you very much.''

Rafe didn't want to think about her getting married, either, although he wasn't about to explore that. As far as he was concerned it was hands off—regardless how much he wanted her.

''You never know what kind of prince the king might dig up. And I do mean prince.''

Her gaze narrowed. ''You know that wouldn't matter to me.''

''I thought all little girls dreamed of marrying a handsome prince.''

''In case you haven't noticed, Mr. Bodyguard, I'm all grown up.''

He'd noticed. Her being all grown up kept him awake nights. ''You're still innocent in the ways of the world.''

She glanced around to make sure they were alone in the hallway, then lowered her voice. "This is about the whole virgin thing, isn't it?" Her mouth tightened. "I can't believe my being a virgin is becoming a bigger deal than it was. I didn't think that was possible."

"Things could be worse."

"Or I could fix the problem. I'm having dinner with Jean-Paul tomorrow night. Maybe I'll take care of my virginity then."

Rafe suddenly found it hard to swallow. "Zara, don't be rash."

"I thought I was just crabby," she told him. "Now I have to add rash to the list? Is there anything about me that you like?"

There was plenty, starting with how she stood her ground when she was annoyed.

She started walking down the hallway. "I can't believe he expects me to simply move here permanently. I don't know that I want to live in the palace. I don't even know if I'm ready to pack everything up and move to Bahania. It's too much, too soon. I need time."

Rafe forced his jealousy aside and caught up with her. "Zara, be careful how you deal with this. The king assumes that you're a new permanent resident of his country. He thinks of you as a member of his family. As such, he considers your place to be here, in the palace."

"What if I don't want to live in the palace?"

He didn't have an answer for that. "Just don't make any sudden decisions. You've spent your whole life looking for your family. Now that you've found one that wants you, wouldn't it be kind of silly to turn your back on them?''

She slowed her pace and nodded. ''I understand what you're saying. I just have this horrible sensation of being trapped.''

Zara hoped Rafe had a few words of wisdom to offer, but when he was silent, she wasn't surprised. He had no experience with her situation. Plus, according to him he'd never wanted to be tied down to anything. He wouldn't understand the ambivalence she felt.

They parted company just outside the door to her suite. She stepped inside and heard movement in Cleo's bedroom.

''Are you finally actually in residence?'' she called, suddenly happy to have someone she trusted and understood to speak with. ''I can only imagine what you've been up to these past few days.''

Zara walked into her sister's room, then stopped just inside the doorway.

Cleo had indeed returned, but obviously wasn't staying long. Several suitcases lay open on the bed. Clothes had been dumped inside, some folded, some not. Her sister moved quickly around the room, picking up toiletries and tossing them toward the open luggage.

''What's going on?'' Zara asked, fighting against the tightness in her chest.

Cleo glanced up at her, her large blue eyes dark with emotion. ''You're the smart one in the family— I would have thought it was obvious.''

"I can see you're packing, but where are you going?"

"Home."

Zara had half expected to hear that her sister was moving in with one of the princes. All of them had paid attention to Cleo, although Prince Sadik had seemed most interested of all.

"Cleo, what are you doing? I thought you were having a good time."

Cleo pulled several shirts out of a bottom drawer and straightened. "I've had a terrific vacation, but I'm ready to head back to the real world. I have a job waiting."

Zara did, too, but she was on summer break, whereas Cleo had simply taken two weeks off from her job in Spokane.

"But don't you want to stay longer?"

Cleo's full mouth twisted slightly at the corner. "Not really. I don't belong here." She motioned to the luxurious room. "You're the princess. I'm just some street kid tagging along."

Zara moved toward her sister. "Don't say that. We're sisters."

Cleo shook her head. "No. Your sister is Princess Sabra of Bahania. I appreciate you letting me share the adventure, but now it's over."

Zara's eyes began to burn. "I don't understand. Sabrina isn't my sister. Not in my heart. I barely know her. Cleo, I need you here."

"I can't stay." She walked to the bed and put the shirts in one of the open suitcases. "You'll be fine. The king really likes having you around. You'll be so busy learning how to be royal, you won't notice I'm gone.''

Zara didn't understand what had happened. She recognized Cleo's determined and prickly exterior as a way to protect herself, but she didn't know why.

"Did someone say something to upset you?" Zara asked.

"No. Everyone's been great."

"Okay. I'll come with you."

Cleo glared at her. "Don't be crazy. All your life you've wanted a father and now you've found one. And, gee, he's a king. Are you seriously going to tell me that you want to walk away from that? If you do, you'll regret it for the rest of your life. We both know that."

"But I don't want to be here without you."

"You'll do fine. You've got those guys interested in you. Hey, you'll probably be engaged by the end of the month."

"Not to the duke," Zara muttered.

"Then to the other one."

"It seems unlikely. You know my luck with men."

Cleo moved close and hugged her. "I would say that your luck is about to change." She stepped back. "I mean it, Zara. I wish you the best. Really. But I can't stay here. I am the last person who belongs here."

Zara knew that Cleo was thinking about her past, about her early years when she'd grown up on the street or in shelters.

"None of that matters."

"It does to me," Cleo told her. "I can take care

of myself. I have a good job. I've worked my way up to manager, and that matters to me. So let me go back to my life and be where I'm supposed to be. You stay here and learn the etiquette of wearing a tiara.''

Zara nodded. She couldn't speak because of the tears filling her eyes. She felt as if she was about to lose something precious, and there was nothing she could do to change Cleo's mind.

Cleo gave her a soft smile, then hugged her. ''Hey, the phones still work. You can call me every couple of days and keep me up-to-date on the royal set.''

''I promise,'' Zara said, holding on tight and wanting to never let go.

Zara found herself barely able to stay awake. The combination of sleeplessness and boring conversation threatened to cause her to doze off in her salad. She blinked several times and took a sip of ice water. Fortunately, Jean-Paul didn't seem to notice her inattention.

''The small flowers are so beautiful,'' he was saying.

She was pretty sure he was still going on about his vineyard. Except for the family chateau, that had been his favorite topic ever since he'd arrived to pick her up at the palace.

''Sounds lovely,'' she murmured when he paused expectantly.

Just then the waiter arrived with their desserts. Zara took a bite of the chocolate mousse and hoped the sugar would give her a little short-term energy.

She was sure that Jean-Paul couldn't possibly be as boring as she imagined. It must be her exhaustion. For the past two nights she'd paced through the large suite, listening to the silence and wishing Cleo hadn't left. Zara had never felt so alone or out-of-place.

She tried to clear her head. This wasn't the time to think about Cleo's sudden departure. She was out with a good-looking French guy who was obviously rich and into wine and vineyards. She should try to enjoy the evening. At least it was more private than her date with Byron. This time there weren't any Hummers or Jeeps. Instead Rafe sat at a nearby table, no doubt trying not to listen.

"You must come to France," Jean-Paul told her. "In the fall, I think. When the tourists have left, yes?"

"You've made it all sound very magical," Zara said, annoyed on behalf of tourists everywhere. Jean-Paul might not like them around, but she would bet they bought a lot of his wine and generally contributed to the economy.

"I remember fall when I was a small boy," he said, sipping the brandy the waiter had brought along with the crème brûlée Jean-Paul had ordered. "I would run barefoot through the leaves. The scent of those days is with me even today. I would take my little dog down to the stream behind the house."

He was off on another tale of his exploits. Zara surreptitiously glanced at her watch. They'd been at dinner more than two hours, and Jean-Paul had spent the entire time talking about himself. The only questions he'd asked had been those inquiring as to whether or not she agreed that his home sounded beautiful. She wondered if he even saw her as a person. Was she simply a single female possibly related to a king? Maybe she could have sent one of Hassan's precious cats in her place. She wasn't sure Jean-Paul would have noticed.

The endless dinner came to a close when the waiter cleared their plates and placed the bill on a small leather tray. Relief coursed through Zara. Rafe was on his third cup of coffee. No doubt he'd needed the caffeine to stay alert, what with being in earshot of Jean-Paul's voice.

She was trying to decide if it would be all right to simply wait outside while Jean-Paul paid, when he startled her by reaching across the table and taking her hand in his.

"Zara, you are an exceptional woman."

She really wanted to ask how he knew. After all, she'd barely said more than a couple of sentences. Instead of creating trouble, she smiled.

He stared at her, his dark eyes alive with promise. "I would very much like to make you mine. I think we would do well together."

She felt her jaw drop. Make her his? Was he offering marriage or simply an affair—and did it matter which?

Annoyance bubbled up inside of her. Did the man really think she'd been charmed by his egotistical, self-centered, boring conversation? That she was available for the asking?

Zara pushed back her chair and rose to her feet.

"I'm afraid you've misjudged the situation," she said formally, her tone frosty.

Rafe moved to her side in an instant.

"I need to get out of here," she told him, ignoring Jean-Paul's protests.

"You're the boss," Rafe told her. He put his arm around her and led her from the restaurant.

Initially Zara was too shocked by Jean-Paul's declaration to notice that they didn't get into the limo that had brought them from the palace. She barely had time to register that they were walking along the streets of the city, before Rafe guided her into a small bar.

The main room held a dozen or so tables, with booths lining the back and side walls. A three-piece combo played on a corner stage. Rafe found a booth in a dark corner and slid onto the bench seat after her. He spoke to the waiter who appeared, then he leaned back in his seat.

"How was dinner?"

Zara frowned at him. Instead of answering, she glanced around the establishment, noting the rich red of the drapes behind the small stage and the inlaid wood that made up the tables. With lazily circling fans and the murmur of different languages, she felt as if she'd stumbled into a scene from *Casablanca*.

The waiter brought two snifters filled with an amber liquid, put them on the table and left.

"Cognac," Rafe said. "You looked like you could use a drink."

She took a sip and felt the burn all the way to her stomach.

"Want to talk about it?" he asked.

"I don't know. Maybe." She leaned back against the seat and drew in a deep breath. "I'm assuming you could hear Jean-Paul's scintillating conversation."

"Even though I tried not to."

"You'll get no sympathy from me. I was forced to sit across from him and act interested."

"So you decided against the great seduction scene."

He was teasing her. She could hear it in the tone of his voice and the light in his blue eyes. She smiled in return.

"I don't think I would have stayed awake for the event." She touched the base of her glass. "This is so much harder than I thought it would be," she admitted.

"What part?"

"All of it. I miss Cleo."

"I'd heard that she returned to the States."

Zara nodded. "She only had two weeks vacation. I'm off for the summer, so my schedule is less pressing. I just wish she'd been able to stay. I liked having her around. I felt more safe with her here."

"Nothing bad is going to happen to you."

She shook her head. "This isn't about being kidnapped. We both know that's unlikely. I mean everything else. When I was little and Fiona would move us every year, I used to dream about finding my father. I always imagined he had a big house with lots of pets and a garden, that he had never known about me and was so happy to see me he held me close and promised to never let go. He told me that I would never have to move again or be the new kid in school.''

"Isn't that what happened?" Rafe asked quietly.

"Yes, and it's terrifying." She wondered if there was a way to explain the fear inside of her. "Tonight was a good example. What was that? Why on earth would Jean-Paul be so incredibly boring and then ask me to be his? I don't even know if he was offering to make me his mistress or proposing. Not that it matters. Does he really think I would be so flattered that I would accept?"

"Maybe he was putting all his cards on the table."

She raised her eyebrows. "You can't actually believe that."

"No, but it sounded good."

She angled toward him. "How am I supposed to fit in with these people? I always wanted roots, but not ones that ran so deep. The king can trace his ancestors back nearly a thousand years. I was thinking more like a couple of generations."

"Is this where I remind you to be careful of what you wish for?"

His words danced across her skin like fire. Against her will, she found herself staring at his mouth, at the lips that had so tenderly kissed hers. While she couldn't imagine having this conversation with any other man she'd ever met, with Rafe she felt perfectly comfortable.

Be careful what you wish for. He was smart to remind her of the danger, because what she wanted most was him. He drew her with a power she didn't understand and could never explain.

"I guess you were right," she said, more to herself

than him. "I'm a wife-and-kids kind of woman. Which doesn't bode well for my life as a princess, should that happen."

"You'll hear within the week."

"I'm starting to regret pushing the king to have the blood test. Now that it's done, I don't want to know."

He took a sip of his cognac. "With most people I'd be assuming they were afraid they wouldn't be a relative, but you're afraid of the opposite."

She shrugged. "I never said I was brave."

"Your concerns about dealing with an entire new way of life aren't cowardly. You're intelligent enough to be able to see the consequences of your actions."

"Only it's a tiny bit too late. After all, I'm here in Bahania, instead of safely back in my little life."

"Sometimes a bigger life is better."

"Maybe."

She wasn't convinced. A bigger life required a different kind of person. Zara had never considered herself very special. If she was Hassan's daughter, she would be a royal princess. The reality of the situation made her palms sweat.

"I don't want to talk about that anymore." She studied him in the dim light. "How did a nice American guy like you become a sheik?"

He flashed her a smile. "Never tell a man he's nice. We hate that word."

"Then I take it back. So how did a mean, surly, very manly guy like you become a sheik?"

"I saved Prince Kardal's life."

He spoke casually, as if giving directions to the airport. She leaned forward. "How? No, wait. First tell me about Prince Kardal. Who is he?"

"Sabrina's husband. He's..." Rafe hesitated.

"This is confidential, Zara. You can't repeat this information to anyone."

His blue eyes darkened with intensity. She felt as if she was about to get the secret code that would save the country from certain destruction. For a brief second she thought about saying she didn't want to know, but then curiosity won.

"I promise."

He studied her as if gauging the value of her word, then he nodded.

"You may have heard of the legend of a secret city on the border between El Bahar and Bahania. The story goes that nomads call this place home. Those who wrote about the city claimed it was a walled wonder filled with treasures stolen from all over the world."

She frowned as bits of history came back to her. "I remember reading something about that. I think I even saw part of a documentary. There are a lot of writings about the city, but no real proof it exists."

"The City of Thieves is real and it's still around today. Kardal is the Prince of Thieves, the next in a long line of men who rule the desert. Back when the silk roads were in use, travelers feared being attacked. The nomads offered protection, for a price. They also stole from those who would not pay. When oil production began, they quickly learned there was more money to be made from the earth than from stealing. Now the City of Thieves guards the oil fields. Using a combination of the old ways and modern technology, we keep the peace."

Zara didn't know what to say. "It's real?"

Rafe nodded.

She couldn't begin to imagine such a place. A

mythical city that still existed? "It would be like learning that Atlantis was alive and well."

"As long as the world doesn't find out."

"I won't say anything," she told him earnestly. "I would never betray your trust." Questions filled her mind. "How did you come to be there?"

"I told the truth before. I worked for a paramilitary organization. Prince Kardal hired us, and when the job was over I stayed on. About a year after that I worked my way up to the head of security. One day we were out in the desert when we were attacked. I saved Kardal's life. In gratitude he made me a sheik."

Rafe unbuttoned the cuff of his right shirtsleeve and pulled up the material. She saw a small mark on the inside of his wrist. Zara leaned closer to study the intricate design.

"What is it?"

"The seal of the City of Thieves. I carry the mark of the prince. As such I own land, livestock and have a fortune, which, while modest by royal prince standards, will keep me comfortable for a long time. They also offered me the woman of my choice, but I turned that down."

Zara nearly choked. "A woman? They offered you a woman?"

He grinned. "Don't you just love it here?"

She glared at him while he fastened his cuff. "That's positively feudal."

"I wasn't all that comfortable with the idea, which is why I refused."

She didn't even know what to say. They'd offered a woman along with livestock? Typical.

"If you're so wealthy with your land and camels and fortune, why do you still work?"

"Because I like what I do."

Rafe picked up his snifter and swirled the cognac. He'd come a long way from his days at the orphanage, he thought. A long way from the scared kid who'd felt so damned alone.

"Do you have any family?" Zara asked.

"No. My folks died when I was four. There wasn't anyone else. I became a ward of the state."

He didn't like to think about his past. He was different now, stronger. He'd learned to take care of himself and never need anyone.

"Why haven't you ever married? There had to have been women in your past."

"Plenty, but I'm not the kind of man who wants roots."

She shook her head. "Everyone wants to belong."

"I don't need anyone else."

"It's a good line, but I don't believe you."

She smiled as she spoke. A pretty smile that made him think about kissing her. Tonight she wore a simple, loose fitting, sleeveless dress. The soft fabric moved with her, both emphasizing and concealing her curves. Her glasses had slipped down her nose, and when she absently pushed them into place, he found himself wanting to remove them and touch her face. He wanted to be close to her, stroke her, hold her. Not just for sex, but for something more.

He reminded himself that getting involved was dangerous. He needed to be free to move on when the time came. However, at that moment he couldn't think of a single place he wanted to go.

"You were never adopted?" she asked.

He stiffened, then forced himself to relax. "I was too old and not cute enough."

"I don't believe that. I'll bet you were an adorable kid."

He'd been quiet and withdrawn. One family had shown interest when he'd been eight. He'd gone home with them for a long weekend. Determined to do everything right, he'd become so terrified of doing anything wrong that he'd frozen up. At the end of the three days, they'd returned him and he'd never seen them again. After that he'd stopped dreaming about things like family and belonging.

"Don't try to make me what I'm not," he told her. "Wishing isn't going to make me different. I'm a coldhearted bastard who has no interest in anything like home and hearth. My home is wherever I sleep that night. I don't need more."

"I don't believe you and I don't think you believe yourself. You've found it easier to go your own way, but in your heart you want what everyone wants. The need to belong is universal."

She was wrong, but he didn't have the words to convince her. "Don't make me into a hero, Zara. I like you, and I want you, but I'll never be the man who can make you happy."

Chapter Eleven

Several days later the door to Zara's suite burst open, and King Hassan walked in trailed by a secretary, a bodyguard and two of the princes.

Zara looked up from the book she was reading and felt a sudden sense of dread. The king's happy expression, the welcoming light in his eyes and the way he pulled her to her feet, then hugged her close told her all she wanted to know.

"It is done," he announced.

She swallowed against a sudden attack of nerves that sent her stomach through a cheerleading routine.

"The blood test results?" she asked in a small voice, even though she already knew.

Hassan released her, beamed, then pulled her close again. "Yes. They have confirmed what you and I have known all along. You are the daughter of my beloved Fiona and my daughter, as well. The joy of my life.'' He put his arm around her and faced his entourage. ''She is the Princess Zara, named for my mother and beloved to me. Let the word be spread.''

Zara felt the floor move beneath her feet. It took her a second to realize that the building wasn't swaying; instead she was having trouble catching her breath and staying upright. Was it her imagination or had the light in the room just dimmed?

Princess Zara? Oh, sure, she'd realized that if she was really the daughter of a king then she was likely to be a princess. She'd turned the concept over in her mind but had never been able to make it real. Nor had she actually thought of herself as ''Princess Zara.'' Did she really have a title?

Instinctively she glanced around at the people in her suite and was relieved when she saw that Rafe had slipped in…probably to see what was going on. She looked at him and took comfort from his wink. He was the only one who could make her feel safe. She couldn't help wishing his arm was around her instead of the king's.

''There is much to be done,'' the king said.

''A press conference,'' one of the princes said. Zara told herself that she was really going to have to learn to tell them apart. If only they weren't all so tall, dark-haired and amazingly handsome.

A third prince entered her room. She recognized Prince Sadik. He walked up and took her hand in his.

''Welcome, my sister,'' he said. ''Do not be too afraid. We will not torment you as we did Sabrina, when she was young.''

"I appreciate that."

The king motioned his assistant to step forward. "We will arrange for a press conference," Hassan said. "The world must know of our joy."

Zara didn't think the princes looked especially joyful. None of this was a surprise to them and they'd all been very kind. She suspected her status as a woman made her practically invisible to them, which was far better than having them outwardly hostile. She wondered how Sabrina would take the news. Although she and her half sister had discussed starting over, they hadn't spent very much time together.

Hassan was still talking about different arrangements. He smiled at her. "You will need a wardrobe fit for a princess. And lands, I think."

Lands? She blinked. "That's not necessary."

Hassan dismissed her with a flick of his wrist. "Yes, lands. Perhaps with oil. Would you like that?" He continued without waiting for her to reply. "There are some lovely jewels that belonged to my mother. As you are named for her, they must be yours."

She slipped free of his embrace. "Your Highness—"

"I would prefer you call me Father," he said, his eyes misting over. "Perhaps not yet, as we are still getting to know each other. But in time. Yes?"

"I—" She swallowed. King Hassan was her father. As in that they shared blood and a gene pool. She had a father.

Her mind spun with the information. It shouldn't be a shock, but it was because now it was real. The room seemed to shift again. Fortunately no one noticed.

"You don't have to give me anything. That's not why I came looking for you."

"I know, my child." He cupped her chin. "But it makes me happy, so you must indulge an old man's simple requests. You are my daughter, and a member of the royal family. Anything less would be an insult to you, to me and to our people."

Her stomach took an elevator ride for her toes. They had people? She was considered...were there people who— Dear God, what was happening?

The next few minutes passed in a blur. More staff members arrived. Phone calls were made, refreshments brought in, questions were asked and answered. The princes all slipped out, but Rafe remained in the background. Zara tried to keep track of everything. She was scheduled for a full wardrobe fitting and a makeover. Hassan called Sabrina to find out the name of her stylist. The wording of the press release was finalized, and all the while Zara had the sense of being trapped in an alternate universe.

Eventually the work was finished. Hassan hugged her one last time before leaving, taking all his people with him. Zara remained seated, too stunned to stand, barely able to breathe. Rafe joined her on the sofa.

"You don't look so great," he told her.

"That matches how I feel." She stared at him. "It's going to be much more than I've imagined, isn't it?"

He nodded. "The circus begins."

The first flicker of fear snaked along her spine. "How bad?"

"I don't know. Just do me one favor. Don't get difficult about having me around. Before I was your bodyguard on the whim of the king. It was a precaution but not necessary. Now I'm going to earn my paycheck."

She didn't like the sound of that, but it was too late to change anything now.

Zara tried to blink normally as the hairdresser snipped wildly around her head. Pieces of dark hair went flying and the low-grade panic she'd been fighting for the past two days increased about 15 percent.

"You look like you're going to bolt," Sabrina said from the salon chair next to Zara's. She took a sip of water from the crystal glass the receptionist had carried over on a tray. "Relax."

"Easy for you to say," Zara muttered.

She found herself blinking frantically again and had to remind herself that eventually she would get used to the sensation of something being in her eye.

"Beauty is pain," Fiona had always told her.

That went double for contact lenses, Zara thought, trying to find the humor in the situation. If only her world would slow down long enough for her to catch her breath. In less than forty-eight hours everything had changed.

Two days ago Sabrina had arrived in her rooms shortly after the king had left. Armed with a secretary and a massive list, they'd gone to work, organizing the first few days of Zara's life as a princess. Their first stop that morning had been at the eye doctor, where Zara had been fitted with soft contact lenses. From there they'd hit several boutiques. She couldn't remember what she'd bought and what had been discarded. Sabrina had done most of the choosing. There had been ball gowns and day clothes and suits and dresses and shoes and handbags.

Zara fingered the fabric of the linen slacks she'd worn out of the last shop. Sabrina had paired them with a turquoise silk shirt and simple loafers. All very upscale and very expensive. She didn't want to think about how much all this was costing. In theory, as the daughter of a king, price shouldn't matter. But she was still Fiona's daughter, as well, and from her mother she'd learned how to stretch a dollar until it whimpered for mercy.

"You can't avoid the press conference," Sabrina said, pulling out the notebook that had accompanied them everywhere. Hassan had already made a formal announcement, and the press were clamoring to meet the new princess. "However, we can limit participation and the number of questions. We'll schedule a few magazine interviews, as well. Maybe one or two weeklies and several monthlies. That should satisfy the public's need to know, at least for a while."

More hair tumbled to the floor. Zara was about to give in to her panic and run when the stylist put down the scissors and reached for the blow dryer.

It was impossible to talk over the hum of the dryer, so while Sabrina made notes, Zara glanced around at the shop. The large open area was decorated in black and red, with white accents. She didn't doubt her cut and style would cost more than she'd spent on food the previous month. After her hair was done, she was to get a makeup lesson and whatever new products she might need. Then she could crawl back to the palace until the press conference the next morning.

As warm air blew over her head, she thought about Cleo. Her sister would have loved the attention and made the situation a whole lot more bearable. But Cleo was back in Spokane, and the couple of times Zara had called to talk to her, Cleo had been distracted.

Three hours later she and Sabrina ate small sandwiches and tea cakes in Zara's palace suite. Dozens of bags and boxes filled the rooms. Stacks of cosmetics and hair products filled her bathroom. Zara figured it would take her half the night to get everything put away.

"The thing is," Sabrina was saying, "you're the princess. You can't forget that. You might have been raised in a relatively normal family, but everything is different. Wherever you go, you represent Bahania. An insult or slight to you reflects on the people."

"I haven't gotten used to having people," Zara said wryly. "I'm not sure they're going to be real keen on me, either."

"They'll adore you," Sabrina assured her. "Just be yourself."

Zara didn't think the people wanted to hear about her rising panic or her urge to throw up.

"You'll need a social secretary," Sabrina said. "I thought I would loan you mine for a few months, just until you learn the ropes. Then you can hire your own.

Depending on how much traveling you're going to be doing, you might also want to think about an assistant. Someone to help with the details of getting your luggage to where it needs to go, packing, unpacking.''

Zara clutched her cup of tea. Sabrina was acting like her staying here was a sure thing. What about her teaching job back in Washington? She'd worked hard to get her doctorate. Was she just going to give it all up?

Her head began to pound. Zara set her cup on the saucer and rubbed her temples. ''I think I'd rather just be the quiet daughter no one knows anything about.''

''I'm afraid it's too late for that,'' Sabrina said kindly. ''My father has told the world about you.''

Zara nodded. She'd seen the press conference on television. At her request she hadn't been there. Her trial would come in the morning. Sabrina had already helped her pick out a dress and accessories. The king was sending over a string of pearls with matching earrings that had belonged to his mother.

Sabrina glanced at her watch and groaned. ''I'm late. Kardal is going to kill me.''

''I doubt that,'' Zara told her, rising to her feet. ''He adores you.''

Sabrina smiled happily. ''The feeling is mutual. Are you going to be all right? I'd stay with you this evening, but Kardal committed us to this dinner, and I can't get out of it.''

''I wouldn't want you to try. You've been so kind already. Go have fun with your husband.''

Sabrina rose, waved and hurried out of the room. Zara sank back onto the sofa and stifled the urge to rub her eyes. Until she removed her contacts, she wasn't allowed to touch them. The last thing she wanted was her new contacts getting lost.

Someone knocked at her door. Zara straightened as her heart began to beat faster. Her first thought was that it was Rafe. As Sabrina's bodyguard had done the shopping—makeover-thing with them, she hadn't seen Rafe all day. She rose quickly and smoothed the front of her slacks. Would he notice the change? She sighed as soon as she thought the question. Of course he would notice—the more important query was would he care?

She opened the door and nearly melted in a puddle on the floor. Rafe stood in the hallway, dressed in a suit and looking good enough to be dessert. No matter how many times she reminded herself that they couldn't possibly have a future and that he'd made his reluctance to get involved incredibly clear, she couldn't help wanting him in her life.

"Hey, Zara, I—"

He broke off in midsentence to stare at her. She self-consciously stepped back. Rafe followed her, then motioned for her to turn around. She spun slowly. As she moved she reached up and fingered her hair. The stylist had cut off about four inches, which had released more waves. Layering and thinning allowed her shorter hair to fall just below her shoulders. He'd blown it out in a soft, sleek style that made her feel glamorous. More intense makeup than she usually wore emphasized her eyes, which were more clearly visible without her glasses.

Between the new hair and makeup and the new

clothes, she felt almost pretty. But it was the approval she saw in Rafe's eyes that convinced her she just might be attractive for the first time in her life.

He gave a soft whistle. "Impressive," he said. "You were something before, but now you're serious princess material." He held up his hands. "Now, the last time a man tried to pay you a compliment, you went ballistic. Are you going to take a swing at me?"

She laughed, remembering her temper over Byron's insincere praise. "No. I know you mean it."

"I do."

He took a step toward her. The pleasure in his eyes turned to fire. Zara's breath caught in anticipation. Rafe might promise that nothing was going to happen between them, but she knew he wanted her. His desire—so thrilling coming from a man like him—made her weak with her own need. She longed to be in his arms, kissing him, touching him and having him make love with her. If that wasn't possible, she simply wanted to spend time with him. He was still her favorite person in Bahania.

"How are you holding up?" he asked.

"I don't know. Everything is so strange. I feel as if I'm caught in the middle of a tornado."

"It'll get worse before it gets better, but hold on to the thought that it *will* get better."

"I hope you're right."

"Hey, don't I know everything?"

She laughed. "Sometimes it seems that way."

"What's going on tonight?" he asked. "I passed Sabrina in the hall, and she said she'd released you for the day."

"I'm just staying in. I have a bunch of stuff to read over before the press conference in the morning."

Rafe nodded. "Want a little company before you get to work? We could order dinner in."

She thought about spending a couple of quiet, uninterrupted hours with Rafe. Although her pulse rate increased, the rest of her relaxed. He was exactly what she needed.

"I'd like that," she whispered.

"Whatever Princess Zara wishes," he said formally, then gave a slight bow. "Mine is to serve."

If only that were true, she thought longingly. If only she could convince him that he was wrong to walk away from relationships. But while the rest of the world might start to see her as Princess Zara of Bahania, she knew that on the inside, she was still Zara Paxton, virgin and unsuccessful graduate in the school of love. Men like Rafe were out of her league. Still, just for tonight, she could dream.

Dozens of flash bulbs exploded in her face. Zara tried not to wince as temporary blindness set in.

"Princess Zara, how do you like Bahania?"

"Princess Zara, has the king given you a fortune?"

"Is there anyone special in your life?"

"Where did you grow up?"

Nearly thirty reporters called out their questions, while Zara tried to keep from bolting. Sabrina had warned that her first press conference would be the most difficult of all. The format was unfamiliar and the members of the press were determined to find out as much about her as they could. Zara did her best to ignore the television cameras in the rear of the room.

She stood behind a podium. Sabrina had suggested the venue be set up that way, rather than with Zara sitting. "Easier to escape when you've had enough," her sister had said, only half joking. "Plus, when it's time to leave, no one will capture the awkward moment of standing and then put an unflattering photo on the cover of every magazine."

King Hassan had been with her for the first twenty minutes, telling how Zara had come into his life and how happy he was to have her with him. Unfortunately a luncheon with the Spanish ambassador had called him away, leaving Zara at the mercy of the press.

There were too many things to remember, she thought as she frantically tried to decide which question to answer first. They continued to pelt her, like small stones. She grabbed the first one that seemed easy.

"I like Bahania very much," she said in a clear voice. Sabrina had told her to take deep breaths and to project her voice, while avoiding speaking above a normal tone. "The countryside is beautiful and the people have been very gracious."

Not that she'd met all that many people, but so far everyone had been really nice.

"What do you think of the king?"

"Have you met the princes?"

"Is the king going to arrange a marriage for you?"

"Right now I'm in the process of getting to know my new family," Zara said. "The princes have been

most welcoming and Princess Sabrina has been help-
ing me with the transition. Without her assistance I
would have run in terror the second I saw all of you
waiting for me.''

Several people laughed, which eased some of
Zara's tension. Still, she would rather have had a root
canal than face this crowd.

She answered questions for about ten more minutes
before stepping back and glancing around for Rafe.
He read her intentions and quickly moved toward her.
After taking her by the arm, he led her out of the
press room and back into the private section of the
palace.

''That was horrible,'' Zara said. She trembled and
found it difficult to walk.

''You did great.''

''I felt like an idiot. Why did all those people show
up just to get a picture of me? And some of the questions seemed really personal.''

Rafe didn't answer. She glanced at him and saw
the set of his jaw. Anger radiated out of him. She
instantly felt small and foolish.

''You think I'm complaining for no good reason,''
she murmured. ''After all, I wanted to find my father
and I did. This is the price of that connection.''

He frowned at her. ''No, I was thinking about those
jackals and how different your life is going to be now.
You think it's going to be easy to return to your old
world, but you're wrong. Nothing is ever going to be
simple again.''

His words didn't make her feel any better. While
she appreciated his concern for her, she had a bad
feeling he was telling the truth about all the changes

she would have to endure. As for not going back to her old life—she couldn't think about that now.

"I miss Cleo," she said as they walked toward her rooms. "I wish she was still in Bahania."

Rafe didn't answer, and she didn't expect him to. After all this was her problem. She'd created it, and now that it existed, she didn't have anyone else to blame.

Zara had never thought about what went into shooting a magazine cover. Maybe the model would try on a few different dresses and use different poses. The photographer would snap a few dozen pictures and it would be done.

She couldn't have been more wrong.

It was nearly four in the afternoon, and the shoot had started shortly after eight. Zara hadn't realized that changing clothes, getting her hair styled and standing, sitting and reclining in different positions would be so tiring. Plus she felt like a fraud. She was hardly model material. All the makeovers in the world weren't going to make her into a beauty. She supposed the only thing she had in common with those who usually graced magazine covers was that she was naturally thin. Somehow she thought the world might be expecting more.

She glanced over and saw Rafe talking on his cell phone. He accompanied her to the shoot. Although he'd stayed in the background, she'd been aware of his presence, and it made her feel better. Of course, this was the easy part. In a week or so she was going to have a one-on-one interview with a writer for the story in the magazine. Sabrina had offered to sit in to guide Zara.

A stylist adjusted the collar of Zara's shirt, then moved one lock of hair. The photographer—invisible behind bright lights—called out for her to "smile pretty."

Zara obliged. She heard the rapid clicking of the camera. She tilted her head when told, raised her chin, thought of something fun she liked to do and prayed for it all to end soon. She was hungry, thirsty and wishing she'd stayed back in the States.

An hour later she was free to go.

"I saw an open-air market," Zara said as she slid into the sleek sports car Rafe had driven them in that morning. "Would it be all right for us to stop there on our way back?"

He hesitated only a moment. "Sure. It's late enough that it shouldn't be crowded."

He eased the car into the afternoon traffic. Zara sank back into the soft leather seat.

"I feel as if I spent the entire day working out in the fields, which is crazy. All I did was pose for a few pictures."

"It looked like hard work."

She flashed him a smile. "I suspect you're just being nice, but I really appreciate the gesture."

"Ready to trade in your day job for a life as a fashion model?"

"Not exactly. I love teaching."

"Tell me about some of your classes."

She laughed. "Rafe, I teach women's studies. You'd hate it. The only guys who attend my classes either think it's an easy way to get a good grade or they're there to pick up girls."

"Maybe I'm a closet feminist."

"Yeah, right."

"I do think women are just as capable as men."

"We all genuflect in thanks."

"Hey, I'm trying to be a sensitive guy, here. You should encourage me."

He pulled into a side street and parked. Zara climbed out of the car and breathed in the scent of the city. She could smell a hint of the sea and several exotic spices. Overlaying everything was the intense heat of the summer afternoon. The air seemed to scorch her lungs with each breath. Yet she didn't want to head back to the palace—not just yet. A few minutes in the marketplace would help her forget the feeling of being trapped.

Rafe moved next to her and pointed to the corner. "We turn left there. The souk stretches about three blocks. Don't try anything fancy. You don't want to get lost here."

She linked her arm with his as they walked. "I don't even want to get lost anywhere. Am I expected to bargain?"

"Usually. They'll go easy on you because you're American."

She started to tell him that she didn't need any special favors, but then reminded herself that she'd never bargained in a market place in her life.

Anticipation filled her as they approached the open-air bazaar. Dozens of people clustered around rows of stalls, moved in groups or stood talking. The stone street looked smooth, as if generations had walked here before. Behind the individual displays, old buildings cast shadows in the late afternoon.

Zara glanced through an open archway and saw two young children playing in a fountain. A small dog danced around, barking. Laughter drifted to her, making her smile.

Up ahead she saw a great pile of rugs. They hung over lengths of rope and chairs. Several stood rolled up in a plastic trash can. To her left was a man selling all kinds of fruit. Everything from dates to bananas to small melons. A display of brass pots caught her attention. She picked up one shaped like Aladdin's lamp.

"Going to give it a good rub?" Rafe asked.

She laughed. "First I'd have to figure out what I was going to wish for."

The shopkeeper moved closer. "It is a fine ornament," he said. "If you're looking for something more functional, I have lanterns that work. If the lady would be so kind as to step around here?"

He motioned to the side of his stall. Zara started to move, but as she did she bumped into someone. She glanced at the teenager and smiled.

"Excuse me."

The girl, maybe sixteen or seventeen with beautiful long dark hair and wearing shorts and a T-shirt, squinted at her.

"It's all right. I wasn't looking—" The teenager gasped. "Oh, my God! It's you." She shrieked. "Princess Zara."

Rafe swore under his breath. Zara didn't understand the problem. She turned to ask him, only to find herself suddenly swept away by a crowd that had formed from thin air.

People surrounded her, tugging on her sleeves, touched her hair, yelling out questions. It was far worse than the press conference, because she felt herself being pushed and jostled. Then someone actually pulled several strands of hair free. Hands turned into claws. She was bumped from behind and nearly went down, all the while trapped in the center of a screeching cacophony.

"Princess Zara, come to my house for dinner."

"Princess Zara, you have to meet my son."

"Princess Zara, are you really from America?"

"Isn't she pretty?"

"I thought she looked better on television."

Words and phrases swirled around her. Zara tried to fight her way free, but she didn't know which direction to go. She couldn't breathe and she had a bad feeling that if she lost her footing, she would be trampled. Tears burned in her eyes.

Suddenly a strong arm encircled her waist. She instantly recognized the heat and scent of the man she couldn't see, and she relaxed as Rafe half carried her away. He pushed and shoved as necessary. One second she'd feared for her life, and the next he was easing her into the car and they were racing away.

"Are you all right?" he asked.

She tried to answer. It was only when the words stuck in her throat that she realized she was sobbing. She covered her face with her hands.

"I can't do this," she breathed. "You have to get me out of here. Get me away from Bahania."

Chapter Twelve

Zara woke in a room on the edge of the world. Sunlight spilled over a pale tile floor. Large French doors stood open, allowing a soft sea breeze to sweep over her, beckoning her. She rose and crossed to the stone patio, then leaned against the iron railing. From there she could see down into the deep, dark ocean, which lapped up against the rocks of the island.

Except for the call of a few birds, the ocean and the breeze, there was only silence. Blissful silence. No servants, no members of the press, not even a relative of the Bahanian royal family.

Zara returned to her room where she showered and dressed, ignoring her contacts in favor of her familiar glasses, then went to explore the house Rafe had brought her to the previous evening. As she'd barely been able to stop crying, she hadn't seen much when their helicopter had landed. She'd been too caught up in trying to get herself together. In the past she'd never considered herself prone to hysterics, but she'd sure been close to falling apart.

Her bedroom emptied into a hallway. Three more bedrooms stood at this end of the house. Rafe's room was next to hers, and a quick glance in the open door showed that he'd awakened before her. Down the hall she found a large living area, with views of the open ocean. To her left was a kitchen with an eating area, to her right a large patio. She saw Rafe sitting at a table in the shade, reading the paper and drinking coffee. Barefoot, she walked out to join him.

"Morning," he said, putting down the paper as she approached. "How are you feeling?"

She sank into the chair next to his and sighed. "Don't sound worried. I have no intention of losing it again anytime soon."

"I'm not worried."

She smiled. "You're lying and I thank you for it." Her smile faded. "I can't begin to tell you what happened at the souk."

"You were attacked by a mob and you didn't like it. That's hardly a surprise."

He made it sound so reasonable.

"Thanks for rescuing me," she said.

"I'm sorry things got out of hand in the first place. I should have been paying closer attention. Or not have let you even go shopping. I didn't think people would figure out who you were so fast."

"Neither did I."

A small, dark-haired woman appeared with a tray.

She set a fresh coffee carafe on the table, along with two bowls of fruit and a platter of hot scones and muffins.

"Enjoy," she said with a slight bow and left.

Zara poured herself some coffee and took a grateful sip. "So where exactly are we?"

"On an island in the Indian Ocean. It's the private property of the king of El Bahar."

She frowned. "El Bahar is next to Bahania, right?"

"Yes. I know King Givon from his frequent visits to the City of Thieves. When you needed to get away, I called and asked if we could borrow his island. Actually we're in one of the smaller houses. There are a couple of larger residences on the other side of the island."

She forced her mouth to stay closed. "Of course. How clever of you to think to call the king of El Bahar. I'm sure if I hadn't been so upset, I would have thought of it, too."

He looked at her. "What?"

She sighed. "My life has changed so much that I have a bodyguard who is friendly enough with a ruling monarch to ask him personal favors. I don't think I want to know where you got the helicopter."

"Hey, you're the one who's a princess, so I don't think you have reason to be picking on me."

"You have a point."

She bit into one of the scones and moaned softly. The flaky treat actually melted on her tongue. While Rafe ate his breakfast, she stared out at the water. She was really on an island in the middle of the Indian Ocean. Six weeks ago she'd been grading final exams in her small two-story town house. A big outing for her was a movie in the neighboring town. Every couple of weeks she headed up to Spokane to spend the weekend with her sister. What on earth was she doing here?

She set down her scone. "I don't think I can do it."

"Do you want to be more specific?"

"I mean all of it. Adjust, be happy, live in Bahania."

"You'd be giving up a lot if you just walked away."

She didn't want to think about that. "Why couldn't my father have been a regular guy?" she asked sadly. "A banker, maybe, or an electrician. Someone normal."

"Sorry. Your dad's the king."

Panic threatened. "When do we have to go back?"

"Not until you're ready. I spoke to Hassan this morning. He would like you to call him when you feel up to it. Just make sure you're all right. While he doesn't understand, I convinced him that you need a few days to get used to all that's happened. He's willing to give you time to adjust to the situation."

"Thank you."

She found herself wanting to reach out and take Rafe's hand. Not only in gratitude, but because he was her anchor in her rapidly drifting world. As long as he was around, she knew she would be safe.

"So it's really okay for us to stay here for a while?" she asked.

''I think you need at least two weeks to relax and sort things out.''

That sounded heavenly. ''But what about your other job? Aren't you due back in the City of Thieves?'' She didn't want to think about being without him, but she had to be practical.

''Kardal can do without me for a little longer. We'll just hang out while you figure out what you want to do.''

Zara shifted on her lounge chair and sipped her icy drink. A girl could get used to this kind of life, she thought as she gazed at the man swimming the length of the pool.

As usual, Rafe was an expert at everything he did. His smooth, clean stokes barely ruffled the surface of the water, while his long, hard, nearly naked body had her hormones doing the hula. He flipped underwater when he reached the far end of the pool and started back.

She supposed she, too, needed exercise, but just the thought of stirring from her chair made her tired. In the past week she'd done little more than eat, sleep, sunbathe and take long walks with Rafe. Except for a very discreet staff, they were alone on the island. She spoke daily with her father and had phoned Cleo a couple of times. Other than that, she had no contact with the outside world.

''You're looking thoughtful about something,'' Rafe said as he pulled himself out of the pool.

He wore boxer-style trunks and nothing else. The man had a fine body, she thought longingly, wishing he'd been as willing to sweep her away sexually as he had been to help her escape Bahania. Obviously, the sight of her skinny body in a one-piece tank suit did nothing to stir his manly desires.

"Just enjoying my life away from the fast lane." She squinted up at him. "Although you must be getting bored."

"Nope. This is my idea of a perfect vacation."

He settled into the chair next to hers. Zara straightened and swung her legs over the side so that she sat facing him.

"Aren't you ready to go back to work for Prince Kardal?"

He glanced at her. "I'm not in a rush," he said. "Are you concerned about Kardal getting annoyed?"

"No." Actually she hadn't thought that at all. "I just wondered if you usually take time off. You strike me as a man who enjoys keeping busy."

He frowned slightly. "I don't take many vacations, except when I'm between assignments or jobs. Then I take about a month and go somewhere like this." He glanced around at their private balcony over the sea, then grinned. "Okay, so it's not *this* nice."

"I know what you mean."

"When I move on, I'll find some island somewhere and flake out for a while."

She frowned. "What do you mean, when you move on? Why would you leave?"

"I always leave. I like change."

She couldn't imagine such a thing. Routine made her comfortable. "Are you looking for a job away from the City of Thieves?"

"I will eventually." He picked up his iced tea and took a drink. "It's been a few years. I should probably start thinking about trying something new."

"But you like it there."

"I'm not the one looking for roots."

"Of any kind." She rested her forearms on her thighs. "I don't understand. Haven't you ever wanted any of the normal things? A wife, kids, stability? Why didn't you ever get married?"

He waited a long time before he answered. After setting down his drink, he smoothed his short hair back and reached for his sunglasses.

"I don't believe in happy endings," he said flatly.

"What?"

He shrugged. "You can't grow up the way I did and think it's going to work out."

She remembered what he'd told about his past. Being orphaned young enough to have trouble recalling his parents yet old enough to be difficult to place. No family had ever taken him home and made him theirs. Had he felt love even once since his parents died?

Zara felt suddenly cold, and shivered. What would life be like if no one had loved her? Fiona had made her crazy at times and had been a somewhat absent-minded parent, but Zara'd had no reason to doubt her love. Plus she had Cleo. She knew her sister would do anything for her. Growing up they'd always been moving around, but the love had been a permanent fixture.

Rafe hadn't had that advantage. In his world love had died early and had never been replaced.

"Wasn't there just one girl who made you want to

stick around?'' she asked, desperately needing to think there *had* been without being sure why.

''No. There have been women, but no one long-term.''

Her chest tightened. In her mind Rafe was a stable force in her life. Yet from all he said, he was just waiting until it was time to move on. Not exactly a formula for happiness.

Zara set her glasses on the table between them, rose and walked to the edge of the pool. She sat on the warm stones and put her bare feet in the water. She ached and couldn't explain why. She knew her pain was about Rafe and the loneliness he'd known, but there was more. Sadness overwhelmed her as she realized he wasn't just holding back because of his job. He was holding back because that's how he lived his life. He didn't want the one thing she'd dreamed of her entire life—roots. He didn't want love. He didn't want forever.

She realized that in the back of her mind, she'd been assuming it was all an act. That somehow he would maybe, possibly come to care about her. She'd been comforted by him, teased by him, made safe by him. For her his actions had been meaningful. But for him... She shook her head. She just didn't know.

Rafe saw the slump in Zara's shoulders and knew that he'd hurt her, although he couldn't say why. Or maybe he could. She might be a successful professor and more intelligent than most, but in her heart, she was still an innocent. She didn't want to hear about the ugliness of his world, or his decision to never get involved.

For a second he toyed with the idea of telling her she was the closest he'd come to breaking his own rules. Her genuineness, her kindness, her ability to make him laugh all drew him. But he knew what would happen if he gave in. Disaster—for both of them. Better not to start something he couldn't finish.

Which solved one problem, but not another. Zara slipped into the pool, gasping at the contrast of the cool water and the hot afternoon sun.

"You didn't tell me the pool was fed by iceberg runoff," she accused.

"I didn't know you were such a sissy."

She tried to splash him but his chair was too far away and the spray fell harmlessly onto the stone patio.

His teasing had done what he'd wanted—she now smiled, and the worry was gone from her eyes. He allowed his gaze to drift over her body. The one-piece suit left nothing to the imagination. He could see every curve, every luscious line. Her small breasts strained against the fabric, making him want to peel down her suit and caress her there. He could see the outline of her nipples, and his lips ached to taste those tight points.

Living in such solitude for the past week had been pure hell. He wanted her and couldn't have her. He ached. Sleep had become impossible because he knew she was close. The servants went home each evening, so there was no one around. No one to stop him. The only thing that kept him from going to her was the knowledge that she deserved someone able to give her what she wanted. All he could promise was a night of passion. For many that would be enough, but Zara deserved so much more.

Rafe knew better than to drink while on duty—or in this case, while in danger of giving in to temptation. But when Zara offered him wine with dinner, he found himself holding out his glass.

She looked great, he thought, studying the way she'd piled her hair up on her head. Once they'd arrived on the island, she'd given up her contact lenses in favor of her glasses. He liked her both ways, so he found her just as attractive as she pushed her glasses into place with an absent gesture he found endearing.

A sleeveless sundress left her arms bare, and two undone buttons allowed him to see the shadow between her breasts. Her skin had tanned to the color of honey. Her feet were bare, her smile easy. She looked like a sensual goddess, risen from the ocean to tempt mankind. He knew he was tempted, nearly beyond reason.

He wanted to tell himself that it was just because he hadn't been with a woman in a long time. That his need was about circumstances and not the least bit specific. But he knew he was lying. He wanted Zara in his bed. Another warm body wouldn't work. He needed to taste her and inhale the sweet scent of her body. He ached to hold her close and bury himself inside of her again and again.

Zara leaned back in her chair and smiled at him. ''You look terribly intense. What are you thinking about?''

He thought about lying. The sunset was beautiful,

as it had been every night. The food left in covered
trays by the servants who had just departed for home
smelled delicious. There were a thousand things he
could say instead of the truth.

"That I'm an idiot."

Zara laughed. "I have to tell you, I wasn't expecting that one. Want to share the reason, or is this because you're a guy."

He shook his head. "It's not, although the two are
related."

He took a drink of his wine. The chardonnay had
a hint of butter blended with the oaky fruit. He could
feel the danger all around him. It wasn't just that he'd
been entrusted with keeping her safe, it was that she
was an innocent. He was hardly the right man to deal
with that. And yet...

"Exactly how much of a virgin are you?"

Zara hadn't been expecting that question. She instantly blushed, which made her feel stupid and im-
mature, but at the same time delight tingled all
through her body. "Are you asking for specifics?"

"Yeah. How far, how often, that sort of thing."

Her heart hammered in her chest. She tried to read
Rafe's expression, but it wasn't easy. Still, he
wouldn't be asking if he wasn't interested, right?
Maybe he was finally going to give in to all that heat
they generated when they were together.

She cleared her throat. Her palms were suddenly
damp, and she knew that if she tried to stand, her legs
would promptly dump her on her butt.

"Well, there was that time in Billy's car. I guess I
was about nineteen. We'd been going out for a while

and he'd had his hand up my blouse.'' She took a quick drink of wine, hoping the alcohol would work fast and give her courage. "As we, ah, maneuvered into position, my foot kinda got caught in the steering wheel. The horn went off. It wouldn't stop until Billy disconnected it from the battery.''

Rafe stared at her. "You're kidding?''

"No. It was a real mood breaker, let me tell you.'' She smiled at his look of disbelief. "I told you—I've had really bad luck in the man department. At least sexually.''

"Zara, your fiancé was gay. I would say your bad luck stretched to more than just sex.''

She ducked her head. "If you're trying to make me feel better, you're doing a lousy job.''

"Sorry.''

"No. You're right.'' She sighed, remembering that night with Billy. "We didn't go out again. I guess he was really mad about his car and embarrassed, too. We'd gotten as far as him unzipping his pants and me, well—'' she took another drink of wine "—I touched it for a second.''

The corners of Rafe's mouth twitched. "It?''

"You know *exactly* what I mean.''

"Okay. Who else?''

"Steve. We dated for a while. He actually touched me, you know, there. I don't know—he was really rough and it didn't feel good. But I wanted to know so I figured we'd go ahead. This was a couple of years after Billy. Anyway, he lived in a really small apartment, but at least it was private. We were both pretty close to naked and I was just about to catch my first glimpse of, you know, when his parents walked in.''

She closed her eyes as the memory and the humiliation washed over her. "He'd given them a key and they were bringing back his laundry.'' She opened her eyes and looked at Rafe. "Can you believe he actually took his dirty clothes back home and his parents delivered them to him when they were clean? Geez.''

She took another drink of wine and cleared her throat. "So, that sort of broke the mood. Then his mother called me and said he had recently broken up with his girlfriend of five years and did I know he was on the rebound.'' She grimaced. "I didn't see Steve after that. I figured that whether or not he was still getting over his ex-girlfriend, the bigger problem was his parents. They were way too involved with his life.''

Rafe looked at her. "I have to tell you, I don't know what to say to that.''

"I know.'' She sighed. "It's really sad. There were a couple of other guys, with equally disastrous results. Then Jon. I've told you about him. After that I just had a series of short-term relationships that ended when the guys found out I was a virgin.''

She looked at him hopefully. "I don't suppose you're asking because you've changed your mind?''

Rafe hesitated, then he glared at her. "You have to know you're a hell of a temptation,'' he growled. "We're stuck on this damned island with no chaperons. You spend your days practically naked, flaunting yourself in front of me.''

She gasped at the unfairness of the accusation, not

to mention her excitement at the fire in his eyes. "I don't flaunt anything. My one-piece bathing suit is incredibly conservative. It's not like I'm this big-chested babe going topless."

He stood up abruptly and crossed to the balcony. Like nearly every room in the house, this one opened onto a view of the sea. Rafe grabbed the metal railing and held on so tightly she could see his knuckles go white.

"I can't even blame it on the wine," he grumbled. "I haven't finished my first glass."

She was both confused and hopeful. "Blame what?"

He spun to face her. Involuntarily her gaze dipped to below his waist. He wore khakis and a short-sleeved shirt. Even with her inexperience, she was able to see all was not as it should be. He seemed to be very...large and very...aroused.

He wanted her. She knew it with a certainty she couldn't explain. Contentment stole over her. Rafe. Always Rafe. He would make everything right, she thought happily. He would be gentle yet sexy and aggressive. He was experienced enough to make her first time good. She trusted him. More important, she wanted him.

"Don't look at me like that," he told her in a low voice.

"Like what?"

"Like I could save the world."

"Oh, I wasn't thinking that at all." She rose to her feet. "I was thinking maybe we could play dangerous sheik and the harem girl. After all, except for my relatives, you're the only sheik I've ever met. I'll probably never get another chance.''

His jaw tightened. She watched him struggle between conscience and need. She couldn't believe that this wonderful, amazing, powerful man actually wanted her. Still, she wasn't stupid enough to question her good fortune.

''This can't mean anything,'' he said at last, taking a single step toward her.

She couldn't help smiling. ''Of course not.''

''I mean it, Zara. I'm not interested in engaging my heart. Don't try to make this more than it is.''

He continued to move toward her, stopping only when he was close enough to pull her against him.

He was hard and hot and she wanted him with an intensity she'd never felt before.

''No hearts,'' she promised. ''Just cheap, casual meaningless sex.''

Chapter Thirteen

Rafe's mouth came down on hers with a kiss that left Zara breathless. Everywhere they touched—especially their mouths—she felt a connection as powerful as the will to live. She *needed* him, needed his arms around her, his heart thundering with the same rhythm as her own. She clung to him as he swept his tongue across her lower lip. Even as she parted to admit him, she clutched the back of his head with one hand, determined to never let him go.

Fire ripped through her as he stroked her tongue with his. Fire and wanting and passion. Her breasts grew more sensitive, her thighs ached. Each breath was exquisite in its perfection, each sensation, each sound. It was as if she'd never lived before this moment.

He broke the kiss and stared into her eyes. His were blue flames of sexual heat that made her giddy.

"What about dinner?" he asked. "We never even got to our salads."

She blinked. "Salad? You want to talk about salad?"

He chuckled. "No. I don't even want to talk about salad dressing."

Then, without warning, he swept her up in his arms and walked into the house.

Zara shrieked as she wrapped her arms around his neck. She felt vulnerable, as if he could drop her at any second—which he could.

"Relax," he said. "It's your first time. I thought I'd give you the whole treatment—you know, carrying you to the bedroom and all that. When some other guy asks about it, I don't want you to have any complaints."

She knew he was both teasing and telling the truth. She didn't want to think about being with any other guy, and thinking about what he was doing and how sweet his actions were brought tears to her eyes.

She blinked them away and focused on the strength in him. When they reached the bedroom—hers, she noticed—he lowered her to the floor.

"Don't move," he said, and lightly touched the tip of her nose.

He disappeared, but returned before she could panic. When he set a small box on her nightstand, she glanced to see what it was, then had to swallow.

Condoms.

On the one hand she appreciated his concern for

her well-being, not to mention the whole birth control thing. On the other hand, were they really going to do it? Now? For real? After all this time was she going to get what all the fuss was about?

She cleared her throat. "I have a few questions," she said.

He grinned. "I figured you might. Ask away."

"You won't mind?"

"No. I'll answer whatever I can."

She couldn't imagine him not knowing everything. She pointed to the box of protection. "Do they work?"

"When used correctly. And yes, I know how."

"When do you put it on?"

"Right before I enter you."

Entering. She'd considered that in the past. She knew what happened between a man and a woman and even knew where everything went. But she'd never been able to figure out how to do it without everyone feeling awkward. They made it look smooth in the movies, but then they were allowed extra takes to get it right.

The sun had set a few minutes before, and the room darkened to twilight. Soon she wouldn't be able to see anything.

"Can we have a light on?" she asked.

"Absolutely." He bent over and clicked on her bedside lamp. "Anything else?"

She had about four million questions, but this didn't seem to be the time. Except for one.

She averted her gaze. "I, ah, was wondering about

the whole, you know." She made a vague gesture with her hands.

Rafe stepped close and touched a finger to her chin. "You're going to have to be a little more specific."

Heat burned on her cheeks. She couldn't look at his face, instead staring at the center of his chest. "The, ah, end part. Where it's supposed to feel really good."

"Climaxing?"

She ducked her head. "Yes." The word was barely a whisper. "I haven't."

"Ever?"

She shook her head.

She felt Rafe stiffen. "Does that change things?" she asked. "Is it too much responsibility? Because if you don't want to..." Her voice trailed off. If he refused her, she was going to be heartbroken.

He cupped her face and kissed her softly. "Zara, I want to make love with you more than I've wanted to be with any other woman. And unless you have any more questions, I'm about to prove it to you."

"I'd like that."

Her words sounded brave, but she was suddenly immobilized by nerves. What did he expect from her? Should she make it more clear that she was clueless? It was humiliating to be her age and so incredibly inept.

Before she could speak, Rafe leaned close. He kissed the corner of her mouth, then her jaw. From there he trailed kisses down her neck. Shivers followed his light caresses, making her tremble slightly.

She rested her hands on his shoulders, as much to touch him as for support.

They'd done this before. She caught her breath in anticipation as he unbuttoned her gauzy sundress. In a moment of boldness she'd never given in to before, she hadn't bothered with a bra, so when he finished unfastening the buttons and pushed her dress down her arms, he bared her to the waist.

"Perfect," he breathed as one hand closed over one breast and his mouth settled on the other.

She gave a small cry as his tongue teased her tight nipple. Sensation shot through her, zipping to her toes, then returning to settle in that place between her thighs. His fingers mirrored his moist touch, teasing her, making her arch toward him, her head falling back, her mouth parted as she gasped for air. When he drew her into his mouth and sucked deeply, she knew she was going to die.

Rafe's other hand moved up and down her back. He must have done something because her dress suddenly fell to the floor. She wore only bikini panties. Even as he continued to pleasure her breasts, he moved his hand lower, over her hips, down to her rear. He cupped the curves there, digging his fingers into her flesh, drawing her against him.

She wanted this. She wanted more.

He raised his head and kissed her mouth. His fingers tugged her panties, drawing them down. She tried not to notice that she was about to be naked, while he was still fully dressed. Then when it was impossible *not* to notice, she tried not to mind.

Rafe kicked off his sandals and pulled off his shirt.

Zara stood there, in front of him. Naked. Just plain naked. She was about to change her mind about the whole sex thing, when he led her to the bed and motioned for her to settle onto the mattress.

It was certainly farther than she'd ever gone before, she thought, hoping humor would ease her growing nervousness. What if she did it wrong? What if he didn't like being with her? What if—

"Stop thinking," he instructed. "I can hear your brain churning from here. Relax. Just relax."

He followed his instructions with a slow, deep kiss that left her breathless. They danced together, their tongues circling, stroking. Some of her tension eased.

He moved his hand to her breasts, touching one and then the other. The combination of kissing and breast touching was heady stuff. When his hand moved lower, she never thought to complain.

"Has any man touched you here in a way you liked?" he asked, trailing his fingers lower down her stomach.

"No."

Rafe kissed her earlobe, then bit gently. "I need you to tell me what feels good," he whispered.

"But how will I know?"

He chuckled. "You'll know."

She doubted that very much. She was the one lacking experience. Why on earth would he expect her to give decent instructions? This was never going to work.

He moved lower still. As he slipped his fingers between her thighs, her legs parted. She didn't remember telling them to do that, but they did. She was about to push them back together when she felt something delicious and amazing.

He stroked her so gently, she thought, barely able to stay conscious and aware of what was happening. It was a lazy exploration, as if they had all the time in the world. She could tell she was already slick by the way his fingers moved easily. He touched all of her—that place where he would enter her later, although it still sounded awkward to her, the protective folds, the damp curls. He pressed in a little, as if searching for something. As if—

She gasped as a bolt of lightning exploded inside of her.

''I would say that's it,'' he murmured and shifted so he was kissing her again.

It? What it?

Zara struggled to figure out what was going on, but it was all too amazing. The more he moved his fingers against her, the more the lightning explosions continued. Her legs fell open more. She wanted to beg him to never stop. She wanted to offer herself as his slave forever. She wished she had state secrets to spill. Anything to keep him touching her.

She knew enough about biology to realize there were nerve endings down there all bundled together with the seemingly sole purpose of bringing her pleasure. She'd just always assumed that part of her body was broken. What a thrill to find out it was alive and functioning extremely well.

How perfectly he touched her. Over and around. Moving evenly, never pressing too hard. His ministrations quickened slightly and she felt herself tensing.

When he broke the kiss to move to her breasts, she caught her breath in anticipation. His touch there had been amazing before, but in combination, it would be exquisite. She had a brief thought that he'd asked about instructions. No way would she be able to speak. Not when he was about to—

She screamed.

His lips came down on her tight nipple, his tongue teased her flesh, then he sucked. It was too much. Deep in her body tension spiraled to the point where she knew she couldn't stand it anymore. Then heat filled her and a hundred thousand tiny convulsions swept through her. She felt transfixed and transformed. She felt perfect and whole. She lost herself in the wonder of her body's ability to experience pleasure.

Rafe's fingers slowed, then moved to her thigh. He lightly kissed her lips. She forced herself to open her eyes and gaze at him. He had a very self-satisfied expression on his face.

"Wow," she said.

"My thoughts exactly."

"So that was what it was like."

"Uh-huh. Although some women take a lot longer."

"That was quick?"

He grinned. "About three minutes. Definitely quick."

She had a feeling he didn't think that was a bad thing. "I had a lot of sex to make up for."

"Apparently. Ready for round two?"

She nodded.

He hesitated. "We don't have to go all the way. You could still stay a virgin."

She shoved him toward the edge of the bed. Or at least she tried to—the man didn't budge. "I don't want to be a virgin anymore. I told you. It's complicated at my age. Come on, Rafe. You can't refuse me now."

"Okay. Just checking."

Just being one of the good guys, she thought, as he sat up and unfastened his trousers. He slipped them and his briefs off before stretching out next to her.

She knew it was rude to stare, but she hadn't seen an actual, well, it, before. She'd touched a couple, but only in the dark.

"You'd see better if you sat up," he said, as if he could read her mind.

She was too curious to be embarrassed. Instead she took his advice and shifted into a sitting position.

Blond hair lightly covered his chest. It thickened at his belly, forming a line that bisected his rippled abdomen. She glanced at the impressive muscles there and made a mental note to start doing sit-ups.

Two scars, one more round than the other, stood out on his skin. She started to ask how he'd been hurt, but figured this wasn't the best time. Then her gaze moved lower to the darker blond hair at the base of his erection.

"I don't have a frame of reference," she said. "Is it big?"

"Huge."

"I'd like to touch you."

"Feel free."

She put her hand on him. He was warm and dry, with velvet-soft skin stretched over pulsing steel.

"Does being so hard hurt?"

"No."

She tilted her head to see between his legs. He parted for her. She moved down to stroke him lightly. From there, she touched his thighs. He had long legs and well-shaped feet. What looked like a scar from a knife cut through his left thigh. All in all, he was a darned impressive package.

"When does the condom go on?" she asked.

"Anytime."

She reached over him and opened the box, then handed him a square package. He opened the plastic and unrolled the protection.

"Did you have to practice that when you were younger? I mean you seem pretty good at it."

He raised himself into a sitting position and urged her to lie down. "It's not a difficult skill to master."

Suddenly she found herself on her back, gazing up at him. Her nerves returned. "I've liked everything we've done so far. Am I going to like this?"

"I'll do my best."

He bent down to kiss her. Before their lips touched, she grabbed his arms. "I should probably tell you that I asked my doctor a few years ago, and she said that there's no, um, physical proof of me being a virgin."

"Thanks for letting me know. That should make it less painful."

She glanced down at his maleness. It did look kinda big to be slipping inside of her easily.

"Don't think about it," he told her, then leaned low and kissed her. His hands moved between her legs.

Now that she knew what to expect, she relaxed into the pleasure that spilled from his fingers. He found that one spot again, but after teasing it for a bit, he moved and slipped a finger inside of her. This was a completely different sensation. He pushed in deeply, then stroked the inside of her.

Her body instantly contracted around him. She gasped. It had been like before, only less intense. Sort of a minisurrender. He thrust into her again, faster this time. She felt another contraction.

Rafe swore under his breath, and she stiffened.

"I'm sorry. What am I doing wrong?"

"Nothing." He kissed her. "You're doing everything right. It's just you're so hot and wet and I can't wait to be inside of you. I can already feel you climaxing. It's your first time and I'm supposed to show a little control. I don't know if I can."

She liked the idea of him being overwhelmed by passion. "Just do the best you can," she said soothingly.

"Gee, thanks."

He moved over her, kneeling between her thighs. He parted her with his fingers, and she felt something thick pushing inside of her. It felt nothing like his finger. Her body stretched in a way that made her uncomfortable—more and deeper until he was buried inside of her.

It was done.

He loomed over her, supporting his weight on his arms. She gazed up at him and felt her heart contract. She'd waited a long time for this moment, and even though the journey had felt endless, she couldn't complain about the destination. This was exactly where she wanted to be.

"Ready?" he asked.

She nodded.

He withdrew and moved back inside. She tilted her hips to help. Again and again he slipped into her, pulling out only to ease into her again. In time she didn't feel quite so stretched. The gentle rhythm grew almost pleasant. Then Rafe reached between them and touched that bundle of nerves buried just below the skin. He rubbed the exact spot in exactly the right way. She felt herself tensing.

It was just as amazing and yet it was different. Better. She liked the sensation of him filling her. She grabbed his hips to pull him closer. He was forced to stop touching her, but she didn't care. She needed more of what he had. More of him.

He lowered himself onto her and kissed her. Their tongues tangled, mimicking the act of love. Pressure build inside of her. More, she thought frantically. More and more and more.

Then she lost herself in a whirlwind of release. She pulsed and cried out and gasped and held on to him as her body spent itself. When she was nearing the end of her journey, she felt him stiffen and call out her name.

Zara opened her eyes to find Rafe looking down at

her. She watched him climax in a moment so intimate she found she couldn't breathe. They held each other close as the last shudders rippled through their bodies.

At that moment she knew she'd lost something more important than her virginity. She'd also lost her heart.

Rafe broke his second fundamental rule when he stayed with Zara into the night. They slept entwined, or at least she slept. He simply held her and stared into the darkness. Of course, when compared with actually deflowering a virginal client who happened to be the long-lost daughter of a ruling monarch, staying in said virgin's bed for the night didn't seem like such a big deal.

She breathed deeply as she slept, making occasional soft noises and cuddling next to him. He liked the feel of her bare skin against his, the scent of her and their lovemaking lingering. When he closed his eyes, he could see them touching each other and re-membered what it had felt like to enter her. She'd been so willing, so responsive, so giving.

He tried to tell himself that the sex had been better than average and to let it go. But he couldn't shake the feeling of having experienced something signifi-cant. He wanted to think it was because she'd been a virgin. He'd never been anyone's first time before, and at his age it wasn't supposed to be an issue. How-ever, he sensed his unease was more than just the fact that Zara had never been with a man before. It had something to do with her having touched his heart along with his body.

As soon as the thought appeared, he dismissed it. Sex, he reminded himself. It had just been about sex. Zara turned him on. He'd resisted and then he'd given in. The situation wasn't any more significant than that. Maybe they'd do it again, maybe they wouldn't—no big deal.

Except he found himself imagining more than just another session of lovemaking. He found himself wondering what it would be like if she was a part of his life longer than—

Rafe disentangled himself from Zara and slipped out of bed. He walked to the open French doors and stood naked in the moonlight. He wasn't going to go there, he told himself. No fantasies about putting down roots and giving away his heart. He knew better. Love didn't exist, except in the most superficial way possible. As soon as it all got tough, people walked away.

He turned and glanced at Zara, still sleeping. He could see the curve of her shoulder and one bare breast. His body stirred with desire. More frightening, something deep inside stirred, as well. As if he wanted more than just sex. As if she'd come to matter.

He pushed the thought away. No one mattered, he reminded himself. Not now, not ever. He didn't do forever or relationships of any kind. He went it alone because that was how he liked it. How many times did he have to learn the lesson that the only person he could depend on was himself?

* * *

Zara nibbled on the mango slice. She felt deliciously wicked, eating breakfast in only her robe. Underneath she wore nothing at all.

"Why are you smiling?" Rafe asked from his place across the small table.

He'd already showered and dressed, pulling on cotton trousers and a loose shirt. He looked dangerous and handsome, and she still couldn't believe what they'd done the previous evening.

"I'm having a good morning," she said contentedly. "Here we are, on a beautiful island, listening to the sound of the surf. We don't have a care in the world."

"You aren't the one about to lose your head."

She dismissed his complaint. "The king will never find out. I certainly don't plan to tell him, so unless you put it in your daily report, he won't ever know."

Rafe drank his coffee. "I don't write a daily report."

"I know, but you check in with someone in Bahania. Just don't mention doing the wild thing."

He didn't return her smile. Instead he studied her. "Zara, about last night—are you okay?"

She knew what he was asking. She'd waited a long time to finally rid herself of her virginity. Was she having second thoughts?

"I'm fine," she said honestly, wishing there was a way to let him know that she was so much more than fine—she was floating with happiness.

Her reaction wasn't just because she finally figured out what all the fuss was about—it was because being with Rafe felt so right. At their moment of completion, she'd realized that she'd fallen in love with him.

Instead of terrifying her, the information had been freeing. All her life she'd wondered if there was someone for her, someone special she could love with all her being. While she'd been engaged to Jon, she'd cared about him and had even loved him, but there hadn't been such a sense of connection.

She felt that she and Rafe would be better together than they were apart. She liked who she was with him and how she felt about herself. She liked that they got along and made each other laugh. There wasn't any fear or regret. Only a strong sense of the rightness of it all.

"Your father keeps asking when you're returning to Bahania," he said. "I figure I can only hold him off for another week."

She sighed. "So you're saying I have to grow up and start thinking about my life?"

"Something like that."

She didn't want to think about real life or being apart from Rafe. Because, regardless of whether she went back to the states or stayed in Bahania, he would be returning to the City of Thieves.

"I have a job waiting for me," she said. "At the end of the summer, they're expecting me to show up and teach my classes."

"You have a father here who wants to get to know you," he reminded her. "I thought you'd come all this way to find your family."

"I have."

"Being a princess isn't just about wearing a tiara. The position comes with responsibilities. Bahania is a growing country, but it's not perfect. There are still a lot of issues for women. Someone with your background could make a difference.''

She looked at him. "You think I should stay."

"I think it's a lot to walk away from. Besides, your regular life is going to be lost to you, either way. You can't go back to being regular Zara Paxton."

She knew he was right. "The thing is, I kind of liked being regular Zara Paxton."

"I liked her, too."

His dark eyes crinkled slightly as he smiled. She wished there was a way to know the right thing to do. She wasn't comfortable with staying, but leaving felt like running away.

"I don't have to decide right now," she said. "I have at least another week." Suddenly her skin felt shivery and hot. "So…what do you want to do for the rest of the day?"

He growled low in his throat. "Don't go there, Zara. Last night was a one-time event."

That was a news flash she hadn't been expecting. "Why? Oh. I know. I read somewhere that men need time to recover before they can make love again, right? So how long do you need?"

He slapped his hands down on the table. "Did it ever occur to you that it might not be smart for us to have an ongoing physical relationship? That it might complicate things?"

At least he hadn't said he didn't want her. "We're both grown-ups." She took a breath for courage. "It's not like we don't want each other."

He stiffened. She could see him waging a battle, but wasn't sure what it was about. They'd already been lovers once, the damage had been done there. She loved him, she knew they didn't have much time together. So why not take advantage of every second they *did* have?

"You make me crazy," he told her as he rose and held out his hand. She put her fingers in his and allowed him to pull her to her feet.

"What about the recovery time?" she asked.

He laughed and pulled her close. "It's not going to slow us down at all," he promised. "Come on. I'll prove it."

Chapter Fourteen

Zara shifted her position in her chair, tucking her feet under her. It was relatively early on the island, but midevening in Spokane.

"I miss you," Zara told Cleo as she held the phone to her ear. "Can't I convince you to come back?"

"I would think you're too busy to miss me," her sister told her. "Or is being a princess getting boring already?"

Zara tried to smile. "It's not that. I'm just so confused about everything and you always know what to do."

"Yet people think you're the smart one."

Cleo's voice was teasing, but Zara thought she heard an edge to her words.

"Are you all right?" Zara asked. "Are you mad at me?"

"No. It's nothing like that." Cleo hesitated. "I just didn't belong there, Zara. You know that. The way I grew up, what I do for a living—I'm the last person who fits in royal circles."

"But you and the princes got along. Especially Prince Sadik."

"Yeah, well, that was just circumstance."

Zara wondered what had happened between them, but she wasn't going to pry. Sometimes Cleo was comfortable talking about her personal life and sometimes she held back.

"Besides," Cleo continued, "you're the one who called me, so you're the one with the problem. You can't be serious about turning your back on the king. He's your father. You owe it to both of you to start a relationship. He's family, Zara. With Fiona gone, he's all that you have left."

"I have you."

"That's different."

Zara had been considering her situation ever since Rafe had brought it up nearly a week before. She'd been turning his words over and over in her mind. Now with Cleo saying everything she'd been thinking, she knew she didn't really have a choice.

"I just don't want to be here without you."

Cleo laughed. "Like you'd notice I was there, what with you and your bodyguard going all hot and heavy. Speaking of which, where is your handsome sheik?"

"Reading on the patio." Zara smiled. "Rafe is so amazing. I can't believe he wants me, but he does. Several times a day. I really like him, Cleo."

"I'd say it's more than like."

Figures Cleo would see the truth. "It is. I love him. I've never felt this way about anyone. I want to spend the rest of my life with him."

"But you don't know how to break through his barriers."

"Exactly. Any brilliant ideas?"

Cleo paused. "From what you've told me, I'm going to guess that Rafe has a problem trusting people to care about him. Maybe no one has. Not since his parents died. So why would he believe you?"

Cleo's thoughts weren't news, but Zara had been hoping for something more promising. "So how do I convince him I'm in this for the long haul?"

"You're going to have to prove yourself."

"How?"

"I don't know. But I think that's what it's going to take."

"Should I throw myself in front of him and beg him to marry me?"

Cleo winced. "That wouldn't be my first choice. I suspect any kind of romantic declaration would make him uneasy."

"I agree." Which was why she'd never even whispered her feelings. Keeping that to herself had been hard. Every time they made love, she wanted to tell him how she felt. Each evening as they dined together, she wanted to speak about her hopes and dreams and hear him respond in kind. Talk about a fantasy.

"There's a good chance this isn't going to end well," Cleo said. "How are you going to deal with that?"

"He'll break my heart," Zara said, knowing it was inevitable. "I love him. I believe I've been waiting for him all my life. I can't imagine a world without him."

"You've got it bad."

"I know. But I'd rather have it bad for him than have it so-what with anyone else."

"That's insane," her sister told her, but Zara heard the love in her voice. "Call me in a couple of days and let me know what's going on."

"I will, I promise. Wish me luck."

"Honey, you're going to need a whole lot more than that. You're going to need a miracle."

Rafe knew he was playing with fire. He could read the truth in Zara's eyes. So far she hadn't declared herself, but it was just a matter of time until she did. And then what?

What was he supposed to say? That he didn't believe her? That he didn't do happily ever after? He'd trapped himself in a living hell. He couldn't have her because he would never allow himself to love her, but he also couldn't let her go. Knowing that she was with someone else would destroy him.

All the tactical training in the world hadn't prepared him for this situation. He'd known the risk to her when he'd taken her into his bed, and he'd done it, anyway. What he hadn't counted on was the risk to himself.

Zara kissed Rafe's mouth. Her body still hummed from the pleasure he'd brought her. She ran her foot up and down his bare leg, smiling at the feel of him.

"You're getting good at this," she teased.

He shifted her onto her back and bent over her. "You think? I could say the same about you, but you were good from the start."

She giggled. "I know. You left out patient. How patient I was with your fumbling."

"Very patient," he murmured before leaning down and licking her right nipple. "Incredibly patient. I should reward you."

Despite the fact that they'd finished making love less than five minutes before, Zara felt her body stir. Just being close to Rafe was enough to get her all hot and bothered.

It was a perfect afternoon, she thought lazily. The overhead fan stirred the warm air. The big bed was comfortable, the sheets cool and the man beside her, touching her, was all she'd ever longed for.

I love you.

She thought the words, breathed them in her sigh, but did not dare speak them. Because she was afraid.

But fear had no place in their bed, so she concentrated on what he was doing to her body and thoughts of equally delicious ways she could pleasure him. Maybe, if she shimmied out of his embrace, she could slip down and take him in her mouth. He always melted when she did that...well, except for the part of him that stayed extremely rigid and got even harder. Or she could—

An odd sound cut through the quiet afternoon. Rafe

raised his head, then swore. Zara strained to make sense of the growing noise.

"Helicopter," Rafe told her as he slid out of bed and reached for his clothes. "Probably Hassan."

It took a couple of seconds for her to assimilate his words. Hassan? She sat up straight. "My father?"

"I guess he got tired of waiting."

The sound was now loud enough for her to recognize it for a helicopter. The change in pitch told her that it was about to land on the pad only a few dozen feet from the house. Then her father would climb out and walk this way and—

"I'm naked!" she shrieked, jumping out of bed.

She lunged for her clothes on the floor, rapidly pulling on her panties. After searching frantically for her bra she remembered she'd stopped wearing one a few days before. For one thing, she didn't need it. For another, Rafe often came up behind her, slipped his hands under her shirt and cupped her breasts. She preferred that contact when her skin was bare.

"Don't think about it," she told herself as she pulled a cotton sundress over her head, then raced to the bathroom to study her appearance.

She looked like a woman who had been well loved. There was no way to hide the color in her face or the contentment in her eyes. Hassan was going to guess the truth.

She hurried back into the bedroom. Rafe had already left. She followed him into the main room and grabbed his arm. "You were kidding about what you said when you first arrived, weren't you? The part about getting your head cut off?"

"He's not going to be happy."

Zara didn't find his words especially reassuring, but before she could question him further, King Hassan stalked into the room, followed by two very tall, very large guards. Behind them were the king's secretary, Sabrina and her husband, Prince Kardal. Zara's stomach dove for the floor.

Hassan stared at them both. Zara wanted to move closer to Rafe and slip her hand into his but she suspected that would not help the situation. There was also the fact that she didn't know how he would react to the declaration, however small. To complicate things, she'd never faced a disapproving father before and wasn't sure how to act.

"My daughter," Hassan said, walking over and kissing her cheek. "The palace has been a dark place without your beauty to brighten my day."

"Hi." She bit her lower lip. "Thank you for understanding that I've needed this time to adjust to all the changes." She suddenly felt really young and terribly guilty, which was strange. After all, she was twenty-eight years old.

Hassan studied her for a few more seconds, then turned his attention to Rafe.

"You will be banished," he said, speaking nearly conversationally, so that Zara didn't catch what he said at first. "At first I thought to have you killed, but Kardal talked me out of it." He glared at his son-in-law. "Apparently, I'm known for having irresistible daughters."

"What?" Zara asked. She glanced at Sabrina who mouthed she would explain it all later. Zara didn't want to wait for an explanation. "What do you mean, banished?" She was going to ignore the "killed" part because she couldn't stand to think about it.

Hassan glared at her. It was the first time he'd ever looked at her with anything but love and devotion. "You have done enough here. I trusted you both and this is how I am repaid. You are new to our ways, so I forgive you, but Rafe has been made one with the desert. He knew what he was doing. He is to be banished for all time. He will not be allowed to set foot in the kingdom of Bahania or the City of Thieves. For the rest of his life he will never see you again, and you will not see him."

Zara turned to Rafe. Not see him? Not ever? She'd resigned herself to being unhappy, to watching him from afar, to dreaming about what might have been, but she'd never thought he would be out of her life forever.

His gaze locked with hers. In that single heartbeat she read a similar anguish in his blue eyes. A need and something more—something wonderful that gave her courage. He cared. She didn't know how much or for how long, but he cared.

"I will not be banished," he said unexpectedly.

He faced the king and pulled back the sleeve of his shirt. She stared at the small tattoo there—the seal of the City of Thieves.

Hassan turned away, Kardal swore, Sabrina gasped. Only the guards didn't react, and Zara had a feeling they were as clueless as she was.

"I carry the mark of the prince," Rafe continued. "At the time I was rewarded and made a sheik, I was offered a woman. I claimed none. I claim one now—Princess Zara.''

He'd never used the title before and it startled her, as did Hassan's sudden expression of rage.

"You will not!'' the king roared.

Kardal shifted uncomfortably. "Must it be this woman?''

"Yes,'' Rafe said, still glaring at the king.

Zara felt lightheaded. Rafe was claiming her as his woman? Did that mean he cared about her? Her heart flew back into her chest and began to tap dance. Hope filled her.

Hassan turned his attention to Kardal. "This is your fault. You allowed him to claim the mark of the prince.''

Kardal shrugged. "He saved my life. I wished to thank him. May I remind you that you are the one who left them alone on an island for two weeks. Obviously, you are no better a father to Zara than you were to Sabrina.''

The king's face darkened. Sabrina stepped between them. "Fighting with each other doesn't solve the problem.''

Zara pressed her lips together. "At the risk of being stupid, what *is* the problem?''

"Yes, explain it to her,'' Hassan said harshly. "Maybe then she won't look at this one with so many stars in her eyes.''

Sabrina sighed. "Zara, when Rafe saved Kardal's life, he was allowed to wear the mark of the prince. It's a great honor.''

"I know about this,'' Zara said impatiently, wanting to get to the "I claim her as my woman" part. "He was made a sheik, given a fortune, along with land and camels."

Her half sister patted her arm. "Exactly. Tradition states that the one who wears the mark of the prince is also allowed a woman. He may take any unmarried woman he likes. *Any* unmarried woman—even the daughter of a king."

Zara was beginning to see the problem. "As what?" she asked Sabrina, although she was looking at Rafe. He continued to glare at Hassan.

"As whatever he wants her to be," Sabrina said softly.

"You see?" Hassan asked. "He is not proposing marriage. He is insulting you, Bahania and even the Prince of Thieves."

Zara took a step toward Rafe. She wasn't so sure insult was his motivation. Maybe it was something else entirely.

"Can you stop him?" she asked her father.

Hassan hesitated. "I am the king. I can do as I like."

"No," Rafe said, turning to her. "He can't. Not without defiling the laws of the desert. He is torn between his relationship with Kardal, his responsibility to the laws of the land and his desire to kill me with his bare hands." He shrugged. "You're the one who was willing to risk having your sex life in the tabloids. I told you we couldn't keep it a secret."

"My mistake." She studied his handsome face, the mouth that had pleased her in so many ways, the eyes that allowed her to stare down into the lonely darkness that was his soul.

"What do you want, Rafe?" she asked. "Is your purpose here really just to tweak the tiger's tail?"

"No."

"Then you really want to claim me as your woman?"

"It cannot be!" Hassan roared. "She is Princess Zara of Bahania. My daughter, a member of the royal family. You insult us all with your thoughtless words and deeds. You were trusted and you turned your back on that trust. You have betrayed us all, especially Zara."

Except Zara didn't feel all that betrayed. She was a little embarrassed to be discussing this in front of everyone and confused as to why Rafe had claimed her, but she didn't feel that he'd let her down. Thank goodness no one knew she had been a virgin. It would all hit the fan then.

"What if I accept?" she asked.

Everyone stared at her. Even Sabrina looked shocked.

"You can't," her half sister said hastily. "You would have no status, no claim. You wouldn't be his wife, Zara. You would be his mistress. As a member of the royal family, you would be dishonored. He could keep you as long as he wanted, then toss you aside with no repercussions. It would be difficult for you to make a good match after that."

Zara thought about Byron and Jean-Paul. It might be difficult to make a good match, but there would be many men willing to marry her.

"I will not allow it," Hassan said.

"It's not your decision to make," Zara told him.

"He will take you away." Hassan stepped forward and touched her cheek. "My daughter, you would be away from your family. You would have nothing. I could not protect you while you were with him."

The light-headed sensation returned. Zara felt as if she were floating above the tableau, watching everyone. Thousands of thoughts swirled through her mind until one of them solidified into a moment of crystal clarity.

She raised herself on her toes and kissed her father's cheek. "I am happy to have found you and I think I could have made peace with my life in Bahania, but this is something I must do."

She turned and moved in front of Rafe. "I accept the honor of being your woman."

Even the guards stiffened in surprise. Rafe, however, simply glared at her. "You can't," he told her. "You're a royal princess. You should be married."

"But that's not what you're offering," she told him.

His glare deepened. "You don't know what you're getting into. I won't stay in one place long. I'll drag you around the world, living in hell holes. You'll have to give up your family. What about your heart's desire to have roots?"

And then she knew. She read it in the pain in his eyes, in the set of his shoulders. After a lifetime of people turning away from him, he wasn't about to trust her with something as fragile as his heart. Not before he knew that she would be willing to stay forever. He needed to test her—and as Cleo had suggested, she, Zara, needed to prove herself.

She didn't know how long it would take. How many months or even years she would have to stand by him until he knew that her love was endless and faithful.

"You're asking me to choose," she whispered. "All my life I've wanted roots—a real family with a history. A father. I have them all now. But I believe love can transcend location. They are my family and will always have a place inside of me. You are my heart's desire. Therefore I will follow you to the ends of the earth if that is your wish. Again, I accept the honor of being your woman."

Rafe stared at Zara, desperately wanting to believe her. He ached as if someone had reached inside and ripped out his heart. He could feel his life's blood seeping away.

She was so beautiful he could barely look upon her. Yet he couldn't turn away. When she smiled, he felt his heart crack.

"I love you," she whispered. "I know I wasn't supposed to. You kept warning me away. I know you're afraid to settle down, so I'll travel with you. We'll create a future and a past that is ours alone. I'm not afraid."

"Zara, you can't." He could barely speak the words.

"I have to. Without you, what's the point? You're all I've been waiting for."

Pain ripped through him. The thick, angry barrier around his heart shattered and blew away. He gasped for breath, then pulled her to him. He touched her face, her hair, then ran his thumb across her mouth.

"Zara," he breathed, and kissed her.

She kissed him back—with all her heart and soul. She clung to him as if she would never let go. He knew then that he had to believe her or lose her forever. That he was nothing without her. That he had finally found a safe place to belong.

"I love you," he told her.

Tears spilled from her eyes. "I was kind of hoping you would say that."

He brushed away the tears. "We don't have to leave. I would never take you away from your family. You just found them."

"I appreciate that, but if you need to be sure, I'll go with you."

"I'm sure," he told her and, for the first time he could remember, he was. Light filled him. Love radiated from them both—he could feel it.

"This is all very nice," Hassan said after clearing his throat. "However, now that you have declared yourselves, I must insist that you marry my daughter. You simply cannot make the Princess Zara your woman."

The king had a point. Rafe took Zara's hands in his. "I never thought I would love anyone, but I love you. I want to spend the rest of my life with you. Please do me the honor of marrying me."

Zara's entire being spilled over with happiness. While she would have done as she said and followed Rafe around the world if necessary, she would much prefer to marry him and make a home.

"Yes," she said, kissing him. "I want to marry you and be with you for always. I love you, Rafe."

Hassan pulled them apart. "All right, all right. Fine. So you want to marry my daughter. What makes you think I'll say yes?"

Zara hugged her father. "Oh, Daddy, what else are you going to say?"

"Daddy," he murmured. "Yes, it is better than father." Hassan kissed her cheek. "I suppose you are right." He glared at Rafe. "I'll expect you to take care of her. She's a member of the royal family."

"I give you my word," Rafe told him.

Hassan sighed. "This is not what I had planned," he told his daughter. "You could have had a duke."

"I'd rather have a sheik," she said happily.

"I can see that. Then I must insist that you promise to wait a few months for the wedding. I want time to get to know you before this one whisks you away to the City of Thieves."

She looked at Rafe who shrugged. "Seems reasonable. How long were you thinking?"

"A year," Hassan said.

Rafe grinned. "Two months."

"Six months."

"Four months."

"Done," her father said. "Four months." He drew his eyebrows together. "Four *chaste* months."

"Not on a bet," Rafe told him.

"I could still have you beheaded," the king said conversationally.

Zara felt so happy, she thought she could fly. She slipped free of her father and cuddled up to Rafe.

They were to be married. All her dreams had come true.

"There will be no beheading," she told her father, then smiled at her fiancé. "That was my first royal pronouncement."

"It was a good one," he said and kissed her.

* * * * *

This Mother's Day
Give Your Mom
✿ A Royal Treat ✿

Win a fabulous one-week vacation in
Puerto Rico for you and your mother at
the luxurious Inter-Continental San Juan
Resort & Casino. The prize includes round
trip airfare for two, breakfast daily and a
mother and daughter day of beauty
at the beachfront hotel's spa.

INTER·CONTINENTAL
San Juan
RESORT & CASINO

Here's all you have to do:

Tell us in 100 words or less how your
mother helped with the romance in your
life. It may be a story about your engagement,
wedding or those boyfriends when you were
a teenager or any other romantic advice
from your mother. The entry will be judged
based on its originality, emotionally
compelling nature and sincerity.
See official rules on following page.

Send your entry to:
Mother's Day Contest

In Canada
P.O. Box 637
Fort Erie, Ontario
L2A 5X3

In U.S.A.
P.O. Box 9076
3010 Walden Ave.
Buffalo, NY
14269-9076

Or enter online at www.eHarlequin.com

All entries must be postmarked by April 1, 2002.
Winner will be announced May 1, 2002. Contest open to
Canadian and U.S. residents who are 18 years of age and older.
No purchase necessary to enter. Void where prohibited.

PRROY

If you enjoyed what you just read,
then we've got an offer you can't resist!

Take 2 bestselling
love stories FREE!
Plus get a FREE surprise gift!

Clip this page and mail it to Silhouette Reader Service™

IN U.S.A.	IN CANADA
3010 Walden Ave.	P.O. Box 609
P.O. Box 1867	Fort Erie, Ontario
Buffalo, N.Y. 14240-1867	L2A 5X3

YES! Please send me 2 free Silhouette Special Edition® novels and my free surprise gift. After receiving them, if I don't wish to receive anymore, I can return the shipping statement marked cancel. If I don't cancel, I will receive 6 brand-new novels every month, before they're available in stores! In the U.S.A., bill me at the bargain price of $3.80 plus 25¢ shipping and handling per book and applicable sales tax, if any*. In Canada, bill me at the bargain price of $4.21 plus 25¢ shipping and handling per book and applicable taxes**. That's the complete price and a savings of at least 10% off the cover prices—what a great deal! I understand that accepting the 2 free books and gift places me under no obligation ever to buy any books. I can always return a shipment and cancel at any time. Even if I never buy another book from Silhouette, the 2 free books and gift are mine to keep forever.

235 SEN DFNN
335 SEN DFNP

Name _____ (PLEASE PRINT) _____

Address _____ Apt.# _____

City _____ State/Prov. _____ Zip/Postal Code _____

* Terms and prices subject to change without notice. Sales tax applicable in N.Y.
** Canadian residents will be charged applicable provincial taxes and GST.
   All orders subject to approval. Offer limited to one per household and not valid to
   current Silhouette Special Edition® subscribers.
   ® are registered trademarks of Harlequin Enterprises Limited.

SPED01   ©1998 Harlequin Enterprises Limited

magazine

♥ —————————————————————— **quizzes**

Is he the one? What kind of lover are you? Visit the **Quizzes** area to find out!

♥ —————————————— **recipes for romance**

Get scrumptious meal ideas with our **Recipes for Romance**.

♥ ———————————————— **romantic movies**

Peek at the **Romantic Movies** area to find Top 10 Flicks about First Love, ten Supersexy Movies, and more.

♥ —————————————————— **royal romance**

Get the latest scoop on your favorite royals in **Royal Romance**.

♥ ———————————————————————— **games**

Check out the **Games** pages to find a ton of interactive romantic fun!

♥ ————————————————— **romantic travel**

In need of a romantic rendezvous? Visit the **Romantic Travel** section for articles and guides.

♥ ——————————————————— **lovescopes**

Are you two compatible? Click your way to the **Lovescopes** area to find out now!

Silhouette® —

where love comes alive—online...

SINTMAG

Silhouette®

COMING NEXT MONTH

#1459 THE PRINCESS IS PREGNANT!—Laurie Paige
Crown and Glory
A shared drink—and a shared night of passion. That's what
happened the night Princess Megan Penwyck met her family
rival, bad boy Earl Jean-Paul Augustave. Then shy Megan learned
she was pregnant, and the tabloids splashed the royal scoop on
every front page....

#1460 THE GROOM'S STAND-IN—Gina Wilkins
Bodyguard Donovan Chance was supposed to escort his best
friend's fiancée-to-be, Chloe Pennington—not fall in love with
her! But when the two were abducted, they had to fight for
survival...and fight their growing desire for each other. When
they finally made it home safely, would Chloe choose a marriage
of convenience...or true love with Donovan?

#1461 FORCE OF NATURE—Peggy Webb
The Westmoreland Diaries
A gorgeous man who had been raised by wolves? Photojournalist
Hannah Westmoreland couldn't believe her eyes—or the primal
urges that Hunter Wolfe stirred within her. When Hannah brought
the lone wolf to civilization, she tamed him...then let him go. Would
attraction between these opposites prove stronger than the call of the
wild?

#1462 THE MAN IN CHARGE—Judith Lyons
Love 'em and leave 'em. Major Griffon Tyler had burned her
before, and Juliana Bondevik didn't want to trust the rugged
mercenary with her heart again. But then Juliana's sneaky father
forced the two lovers to reunite by hiring Griffon to kidnap his
daughter. Passions flared all over again, but this time Juliana was
hiding a small secret—their baby!

#1463 DAKOTA BRIDE—Wendy Warren
Young widow Nettie Owens had just lost everything...so how
could she possibly be interested in Chase Reynolds, the mysterious
bachelor who'd just landed in town? Then Chase learned that he
was a father, and he asked Nettie to marry him to provide a home
for his child. Would a union for the baby's sake help these two
wounded souls find true love again?

#1464 TROUBLE IN TOURMALINE—Jane Toombs
To forget his painful past...that's why lawyer David Severin escaped
to his aunt's small Nevada town. Then psychologist
Amy Simon showed up for a new job and decided to make
David her new patient—without telling David! Would Amy's
secret scheme help David face his inner demons...and give the
doctor an unexpected taste of her own medicine? SSECNM0302